THE GHOST OF MADISON AVENUE

NANCY BILYEAU

Dedicated to Mary Elizabeth O'Neill, my mother

This is a work of fiction. All rights reserved. Names, characters, places, and incidents are either the product of the author's imagination or are used fictitiously, and any resemblance to actual persons, living or dead, business establishments, events, or locales is entirely coincidental.

Cover design by Bosa Grgurevic.

❀ Created with Vellum

PROLOGUE

Manhattan, December 23, 1912

Helen O'Neill pressed herself against the back wall of the dark cloakroom and waited to learn her fate. Her legs ached and her back throbbed from standing for so long—exactly how long, she didn't know. There were no chairs wedged into this tiny space, not even a box or a crate to sit on. Helen refused to lower herself to the floor, though. She couldn't bear to be huddled there like a frightened animal when her employer unlocked the cloakroom door.

Careful and sensible. That was the phrase Belle da Costa Greene used on Helen's first day at Morgan's private library, offered in praise of her character. If before today anyone had asked if she agreed with such an assessment, Helen would've said yes. Yet what she did this afternoon was reckless, it was appalling, outrageous, and ungrateful. She seized a chance and snuck into a room where she had no business being, the private study of financier J. P. Morgan. Desperate to discover the truth, she'd rifled through his desk, searching, searching, searching.

Helen thought she'd slipped into the sumptuous study undetected. But she was no expert in subterfuge. She flinched at the memory of Belle da Costa Greene's expression: horrified and enraged. From the doorway Belle obviously saw Helen standing behind J. P. Morgan's desk, holding the large photograph in its elegant silver frame.

"Are you a madwoman or a thief?" Belle cried. Helen tried to explain. Her stammered denial only made Belle angrier. She marched Helen out of the study and, there being limited places to put a disgraced employee until Mr. Morgan returned to the library, shoved her into the cloakroom and locked the door. "I can't trust you near any of the collections now, and I simply can't bear to look at you," Belle said.

Her time trapped inside had revealed all sorts of bleak possibilities.

Would Morgan terminate her due to this grave offense, no letter of recommendation tendered, or send for the police? The disgrace of that, its impact on her family, made tears burn the corner of her eyes. Her brothers' faces when told? Helen shuddered.

Yet that wasn't the most frightening thing she faced today. It was the moment she held the photograph in her hands, what it revealed. Something impossible ... that *was* possible.

The lock in the cloakroom door clicked. It must be Belle da Costa Greene.

What will happen to me now? she wondered.

Helen pressed her palms even harder against the back wall, as if to melt into it. But there was no escape. This moment seemed so unreal. In her obsession to learn what was happening to her, Helen destroyed a job she'd begun just over two weeks ago, one that had held such promise...

CHAPTER 1

The Bronx, December 8, 1912

"It's a great big terrible nose Mr. Morgan has," said Helen's younger brother, Stephen, not five minutes after the Connolly family sat down to Sunday dinner. "A disfigurement. I understand that if you look at it, the man takes offense and gives you the most ferocious stare."

Now she'd be in for it.

Helen sipped her water, trying to hide her annoyance with her brother. She was the one who would be working for J. P. Morgan beginning on Monday, but Stephen commanded respect from the rest of the family. He was a teacher of Latin, notwithstanding his pupils were pimply thirteen-year-old boys at St. Andrew's Academy.

"Won't you be scared, Aunt Helen, looking at him?" asked little Rose, the youngest of John Jr.'s children, her blue eyes widening over her own freckled snub nose.

Helen set down her glass and smiled at Rose. "I don't know if I shall ever see Mr. Morgan in the flesh," she explained. "He's quite a busy man, and I'll be working for the lady who takes care of his library, not him."

"I'm glad," she whispered.

Helen reached over and patted her niece's silky reddish-gold curls.

Her older brother, John Connolly Jr., standing at the head of the table, paused in his carving of the beef roast and said, "Hear that, Rose? Your favorite aunt is in no danger."

Stephen wasn't finished making pronouncements, though. "The physical disfigurement could be a judgment of God brought on by his greed and the suffering of the poor, all the fault of his bank," he said. "Some say J. P. Morgan is cursed."

What nonsense. And you'd be the last person to believe in such a thing. You barely make it to Mass, and you sneer at the superstitious.

But her teenage nephews seemed interested in the conversation for the first time, which meant John Jr.'s wife, Siobhan, must now weigh in. She crossed herself and said, "Please, there's never cause to talk of curses at dinner."

"Duly noted," Stephen said.

With that, it would seem the subject of J. P. Morgan was closed. A few minutes later, slabs of glistening brown meat adorned each of the plates passed counterclockwise as serving dishes of boiled potatoes, carrots, and rolls circled the table clockwise. It was John Jr. himself who brought it up again, surprisingly.

Pointing his grease-christened knife at Helen, he said, "You see that the man pays you properly. I don't know why I should subsidize Mr. Morgan's payroll here in Morrisania."

"Certainly," Helen said. She realized that her going to work for J. P. Morgan, the giant of Wall Street, famous throughout the world, was on one level a source of pride for the family, but it also carried potential for embarrassment.

They all went to great lengths to support the pretense put on for the children, the neighbors, and their friends that it was

John Jr., a police sergeant in the Bronx, who paid for everything. John Jr. had been head of the family ever since the death of their father in that terrible accident, struck down while building Macombs Dam Bridge over the Harlem River. But it wasn't just his being oldest that made John Jr. the head. Everyone in the family adored him.

However, the discreet truth was Stephen's salary equaled his older brother's and Helen had earned the highest pay of all the siblings for years. Without pooling their paychecks, how else could the Connollys have moved into this two-story clapboard house, with indoor plumbing and electricity and enough land out back for not only a fenced vegetable garden but also a chicken coop? If his two siblings moved out from under John Jr.'s roof, he'd soon be struggling. But another unspoken truth was that there was little chance of such a change. It seemed Stephen would never take a wife and Helen, a childless widow, would never take a second husband.

Helen picked at her meat. If only Siobhan flavored the roasts. Not that she could ever be criticized for cooking like every other wife in their circle. All over Morrisania, Irish families were settling around the table, tucking into Sunday dinner in the early darkness of December. At those tables, the main dish would be hearty in portion but both overcooked and under-seasoned. Helen was the rare one who knew what a sprinkling of herbs or a sauce could do, thanks to her jobs "over the river."

But Helen recognized her restless mood wasn't due to Siobhan's cooking. She had felt out of sorts all weekend. Could it be true that tomorrow she would begin her new position as special cleaner and restorer at the private library of J. P. Morgan?

After five years at the Metropolitan Museum of Art, she'd suddenly learned she had a new job.

"You've being poached," the museum director told her with

a tight smile. "Mr. Morgan is the chairman of the museum board, he's the preeminent private collector in America. It wasn't possible to refuse. Congratulations, Mrs. O'Neill. We will miss you, but Mr. Morgan's private library is quite something, like a temple for his treasures."

Helen knew she should be transported with joy over being hired for a temple. Instead, those butterflies in her stomach were turning into giant thumping moths.

Oh, but this was a ridiculous time for nerves. Good jobs were scarce. Any sane person—man or woman—would be grateful to work for J. P. Morgan in any capacity. At bedtime, when it was Helen's turn for the washroom, she stared at herself in the house's one and only mirror and said, "Stop being such a ninny."

Standing there in her long, flowered nightgown, her robe tightly belted, Helen felt neither chastened nor amused by the command from her mirrored self but as chilled as if she'd stepped onto an iceberg in her bare feet. Thirty-five years old—no, she wasn't young by any stretch of the imagination, but should she look *this* old? Both Helen and Stephen sprouted gray hair by the age of thirty. On Stephen it made for a distinguished profile. On Helen, fading blonde hair made her look nothing but aged, she feared. Even worse were the lines carved across her high forehead and stretching from the sides of her nose to her mouth.

Unbidden, she remembered what her mother said on Helen's wedding day. She'd never set out to hurt her, but there was surprise when Anne Connolly said, "Ah, my goodness, but you look *pretty*, Helen."

And on the heels of that recollection she heard in her head John Jr.'s words. Five years ago, their mother dead, he was drinking beers on the front stoop with a friend and, not seeing her standing behind, said sadly, "She was lucky to get one husband, I doubt our Helen will catch a second."

Helen O'Neill, maiden name Helen Connolly, possessed a flawless memory. Not for the first time, she wished otherwise.

Helen turned away from her reflection and padded down the hallway to her bedroom.

What of it?

She might look like a pale, graying little sparrow, but that had nothing to do with anything. She hadn't been hired for her looks.

Helen settled into bed, pulling up the heavy covers to banish the cold. Suddenly she threw off those blankets and made her way in the dark to the dresser. She felt her way to the back of the bottom drawer, pulling out a little box.

Inside it was an unopened jar of Vanishing Cream, a birthday present from Siobhan. The advertisements for it appeared in all the newspapers: A beautiful woman with thick hair piled atop her head, sitting before a dressing table, holds up a jar to her prim aproned maid, with the words written above: "Mary, be sure and get me another jar of this Pond Extract Company's Vanishing Cream. You know I can't do without it."

Vaguely insulted by such a gift, Helen had not tried the Pond's. She was one woman who *could* do without it.

Yet tonight, she unscrewed the tight lid and dipped her finger into the thick cream. The cool, tingling mask felt delightful on her face and neck.

Like a magic potion.

The word *magic* made Helen stiffen in her narrow single bed. This could be at the bottom of what worried her—the knowledge of having a special talent for her work which had little to do with any schooling or training. She had never understood it herself. Yet all along it had helped her, propelled her forward ... all the way to the private library of J. P. Morgan.

"She's *aes sidhe*," her mother said that day, watching her youngest child, then seven years old, impress the crowd of other children with her gift of the hands. Helen had always loved her mother's voice, the singsong accent of County Cork. But even at that age, she could sense fear in Anne Connolly's voice and the look in her eyes. How could her mother be afraid of her?

I only want to be like everyone else.

It was a longing Helen felt ever since, without the power to change anything.

She slept fitfully until she heard it: *clop clop clop.* Horse hooves on the street, interspersed with footsteps and the clinking of glass bottles, drifted into the room. Mr. Watson's milk route was her signal to rise.

Weary from a bad night but determined to make a good start, Helen was pacing the platform of the IRT Third Avenue Elevated Line, known by one and all as the Bronx El, just over an hour later. A weak sun trembled atop the tall line of trees rising on the eastern horizon. The morning was bitter cold, with gathering gray clouds, the sort that foretold snow. If so, she was ready for it, wearing her new single-breasted coat, a wool hat, gloves, and her sturdiest brown shoes.

A new job called for a new route, with Helen no longer making her way on subway and trolley and on foot to the Metropolitan Museum of Art, rising out of Central Park. Instead she must push farther south to Thirty-Sixth Street and Madison Avenue, into the thick of Manhattan.

She arrived at Pennsylvania Station at its most crowded hour. Could it be any louder in this enormous lobby? And outside on Thirty-Third Street, the jostling of those around her —most of them men and all of them taller—would have unnerved many women. Not Helen. She kept her chin up and her attention sharp.

Helen was especially wary of the motorcars among the horses, streetcars, and pedestrians on the streets. These drivers didn't appear to have control of their roaring, surging machines. She made her speedy yet cautious trek walking crosstown—Seventh Avenue, Sixth, Broadway, Fifth—as the crowd thinned only slightly.

When she reached Madison Avenue, where she needed to turn north, the crowds fell away. Sedate, silent brownstones fronted by tall trees lined both sides of Madison. One brownstone was festooned with holly, in keeping with the season.

It's so quiet here.

The only other person on her stretch of sidewalk was a man and his dog. The man, barely dressed for the cold, wearing a black lounge coat alone, puffed his cigar as he strolled by with an Airedale Terrier. He blinked at Helen twice as he passed her, bestowing as much deference as he presumed fitting to a strange woman alone on Madison Avenue.

They had told her at the Metropolitan Museum that J. P. Morgan, an aggressive and discriminating collector of rare books, valuable paintings, and treasures of antiquity, built a library to house his collection right next to his New York City home. Helen peered up at the bristling three-story brick house, covered with Boston Ivy, which must contain Mr. Morgan and all the assorted Morgans of his family. Surely the man himself was by now presiding at the bank that took his name down on Wall Street. A person didn't get to be as rich as he was—richer than King George of England or even Czar Nicholas of Russia, some said—lingering by the fire at home or fiddling in his private library.

Her steps slowed as she turned off Madison and headed east to what had to be her appointed destination: Thirty-Three East Thirty-Sixth Street. To her eyes, this was no library built to hold books but a miniature palace, fashioned out of pale pink marble with Greek columns soaring. Her heart pounding under her layers of clothing, Helen mounted three steps leading to a recessed platform. In front of her stood tall dark-gold doors decorated with rows of square panels.

My Lord, is this entranceway made of bronze?

There was no doorknob, no handles. How could she alert anyone to her arrival? The thought of knocking on thick, decorated bronze panels made Helen shake her head, a nervous giggle catching in her throat.

The minutes crawled by. She glanced over her shoulder. A motorcar rumbled by on Thirty-Sixth Street; a whistling man hurried by on the sidewalk. All oblivious.

"Open sesame," Helen whispered. When she and Stephen were very young, and her brother captivated by tales of *One Thousand and One Nights*, he would scramble around the house, shouting, "Open sesame" at every door, with Helen, his adoring acolyte, trailing him every minute.

At last Helen spotted a discreet bell to the right and pushed hard, the answering vibration delivering a slightly unpleasant shock.

It was only then that the thick bronze doors eased open, ever so slowly.

CHAPTER 2

A tall uniformed man with a stiff black moustache stepped out from Morgan's library to stare down at Helen.

"Mrs. O'Neill, come to report to work," she informed him, straightening her shoulders. It was always important with a new job to establish her status at the very beginning. When he didn't react, not a muscle on his face moving, she said, "I'm here to see Miss Greene."

With that, Helen was ushered inside. And if the brass doors took her aback, that was nothing compared to the grandeur of the vaulted marble rotunda. Exquisite murals glowed everywhere: on the walls, covering the ceiling. They featured men and women from history, wearing armor or togas or draping cloaks. Helen was accustomed to wealthy Manhattanites' hunger for huge stone buildings that looked like they were lifted from ancient Greece and Italy and flown across the Atlantic, the Metropolitan Museum of Art reigning supreme in that department. But this rotunda was fit for a cathedral—for Rome itself. The Pope would be pleased with such a ceiling.

"Mrs. O'Neill, I'm so happy to have you here," said Belle da Costa Greene, emerging from one of the three doorways opening off the rotunda. She smiled a welcome, her hand extended to shake Helen's.

Young, slender, her black hair artfully arranged, Belle wore a deep blue dress with an empire waist, draped in chiffon. She was as pretty and pampered as the female in the Pond's advertisement. Not the appearance one would expect of a librarian.

Helen whipped off her winter gloves in order to shake Belle da Costa Greene's smooth hand. "Oh, but your hand's so cold," said Belle, still smiling but tilting her head in a question. "I hope you didn't need to travel far to reach us."

"No at all," Helen fibbed.

Belle directed Helen to the room off the rotunda she had emerged from. "This is the North Study—my office," she said, her voice radiating pride.

And rightly so.

The walls of the tall square room were covered in paneling that gleamed the warmest brown possible, illuminated by winter light streaming in from two windows, a low fire in the fireplace, and a bright lamp set next to Belle's large desk. Again, the room's ceiling was transformed into a series of tableaus from history, one exquisite Renaissance-inspired mural after another. Bookshelves were packed with neatly ordered books, hundreds of them.

This room is simply gorgeous, she marveled.

Belle showed Helen where the adjoining cloakroom was, so she could hang her coat and put away her things, and then explained her own role at the library. Six years ago, J. P. Morgan hired Belle away from Princeton University's library in order to take charge of his collection. She cataloged and organized his books and ancient manuscripts and treasures, and, even more important, she was the guiding force in new acquisitions.

"The situation here is that Mr. Morgan's collection is so, well, so *vast*," Belle said, her tone as indulgent as it would be for a boy owning an abundance of train sets. "Not just with his new purchases but the things he's had for years—they need to be assessed and maintained. I have assistants, but none of them with your specialized background, Mrs. O'Neill. Everything must be kept in the best possible condition. Mr. Peterson at the museum told me how careful and sensible you are. I can't tell you how much of a relief it will be to me, what a burden off my shoulders, to know that your skills are being brought to bear here."

Careful and sensible—yes that would be me. Aloud, she said, "Thank you, Miss. I will do my very best."

Helen glanced at the large framed photograph mounted on the side table to Belle's desk. A tall, heavyset, unsmiling older man with piercing dark eyes posed next to a fur-swaddled woman of his age, flanked by three younger women and one man.

"That's Mr. Morgan and his family." Belle smiled. "Mrs. Morgan likes to say her husband would buy anything from a pyramid to Mary Magdalene's tomb."

Miss Greene is not just friendly and polite—she's fun.

Helen's nervousness was melting away.

In a final glance at Mr. Morgan's image, Helen also took note that the man's nose was mottled and drooping but hardly the terror Stephen described. He must suffer a skin condition of some kind.

Belle explained that Helen's working space would be in Mr. Morgan's main library. She followed Belle into the rotunda, patrolled by three uniformed guards, and past a closed set of doors. "That is Mr. Morgan's study," Belle said, pointing an elegant finger. "But we don't unlock it or light the fire when he's not here."

"Is Mr. Morgan often here?" Helen asked tentatively.

"Oh, yes, this is where he prefers to be whenever he is in New York. He likes to handle his correspondence and hold small meetings here, rather than at the bank. He travels abroad six months of the year, of course. At present he's in the United States, just not here. He's in Washington, D.C." Belle's voice turned somber. Helen barely noticed, she was reeling from the news that J. P. Morgan would often be physically present in the same building where she worked.

Next Helen followed Belle into the main library. Incredibly, it dwarfed Belle's office. It was thirty feet tall, as high as a two-story building. Naturally it boasted fine wood paneling and ceiling paintings galore.

So many books! Helen was rendered speechless, trying not to gape at the bookshelves. There were not just hundreds of books and manuscripts here, but *thousands* of them. The room was divided into triple tiers of wall-mounted bookshelves, facing a series of balconies. As she scanned the balconies, Helen could detect no stairs connecting the levels. Nor were there portable ladders leaning against any walls.

"How do you reach the different levels?" she asked. "There's no way to get to the higher balconies."

"Oh, my, you're quick to spot that," Belle said, approvingly. "Come, follow me."

Her heels clicking on the wooden floor, Belle headed straight for the far left corner of the main floor of shelves. She stuck in her hand, seized something, and pulled. It was a long lever, and Belle gracefully stepped aside so Helen could see a tall section of the corner swing open like a door. Inside was revealed a narrow circular staircase spiraling up and out of sight. There were two such sets of interior winding stairs installed, Belle explained. This was the only way to travel between floor and balconies. But you had to know where the levers were to open the staircases.

"We have our little secrets here at the Morgan Library," Belle said. "But I'm counting on you to be sensible about it all. That won't ever be a problem, Mrs. O'Neill?"

"No, Miss."

It's certainly important to her that I'm sensible.

Belle da Costa Greene guided her to her station: a table set up in the corner of the main library. On top was a tray of small objects set under a strong lamp, various cloths and four different-size brushes, along with a bowl of water and some tubes.

"I thought we'd start with the cuneiform seals," Belle said. "They are in need of your attention."

Helen took a seat at the table and removed from her small satchel the gloves she'd brought with her, the ones custom-made for her tiny hands. She glanced up to catch Belle looking down, eyebrows scrunched in worry.

"Is there something the matter, Miss?"

"No, Mrs. O'Neill. It's just that you look so small sitting there—and so, well, delicate."

"I'm very strong, Miss. And healthy, if that is what you are wondering?"

"Oh, yes, I am sure you are. Please, think nothing of what I said."

Helen finished putting on her gloves and, without looking up, said, "It's my brother Stephen who is delicate, not me." The instant the words were out of her mouth, she was horrified. How could she speak of personal matters, of family, to her new employer?

But instead of being offended, Belle laughed, a sophisticated trill, and then launched into an explanation of the five cuneiform seals laid out before Helen. Each was an inch or so in length, engraved in Mesopotamia in the fourth century BC.

Helen picked up the first one, held it closer to the lamp, studied it, and selected the smallest brush, giving it a whisk hardly stronger than a faint puff of wind. "Oh, my," Belle said. And then, "Would you mind if I sat down with you and observed for a time? I find this so interesting."

"Please do, Miss Greene."

Helen was used to people watching her work, sometimes

delighted, sometimes dumbfounded. They all of them sensed there was something special about Helen's hands, her concentrated movements, always so subtle. But none who observed had ever said that phrase spoken by Helen's mother when she was seven years old, and Helen felt safe in assuming no one would.

Youngsters had come from all over the neighborhood to witness Helen's ability with playing cards and Tiddlywinks and, most of all, Jacks. It was her oldest brother who put out the word of his baby sister's talents and, truth be told, even charged some of the gullible a few pennies for the honor of seeing her in action. John Jr. was a scamp, on his way to becoming a scoundrel, before he took it into his mind to be a policeman.

With Jacks, you dropped a little rubber ball and scooped up tiny Jacks off the floor in the seconds between ball bounces, first one, then two, then three, all the way to ten. Few people, no matter how much they practiced, could pick up more than eight Jacks between ball bounces. Helen, with a whirl of her hand, flicked up all ten of the Jacks perfectly, over and over. She could pick up any number of Jacks, no matter how far apart they sprawled on the floor. As the others cheered, she grinned. She enjoyed impressing everyone—and it was so easy!

But Helen's mother, standing in the shadows of the room one day while the children played, suddenly ordered everyone out of the room except her youngest daughter, whom she regarded with that strange fear.

It was only later that night, with her parents arguing loudly on the other side of the paper-thin wall, that Helen learned what the strange words *aes sidhe* meant, which to her ears sounded like "eye shee." It was a Gaelic term for special beings who lived in Ireland, "people of the mounds" who emerged to mingle with human beings when it suited them.

"Those are stupid stories—not in the least Christian," roared her father, John Sr. "I won't have you bringing fairy tales of the bog into our home. It's bad enough you take it seriously, but to put it about that Little Helen might be able to see spirit beings out among the normal people—do special things with her hands?"

Her father was born in New York, in the depths of the Five Points, the son of a couple that fled Ireland in the first year of the Famine that would kill millions. But her mother was born in Ireland and didn't make the journey across the ocean until she was twelve. She held tightly to her heritage. "It's not stupid—it's real," her mother insisted. "Helen has in her some of the blood of the *aes sidhe* and we have to help her hide it. We have to keep her safe."

Anne Connolly never spoke of her beliefs again in her husband's hearing. But she took Helen aside in private and swore her to secrecy. Helen must tamp down her gift with her hands. Just use it enough to be good at women's work, her mother pleaded. Scared and unsure of herself, anxious for her mother's approval, she did what she was told.

Helen tamped it down. She stopped playing Jacks; she avoided all the boys' neighborhood games until they stopped trying to lure her—and John Jr. stopped recruiting an audience. Instead, she allowed her gift to guide her in her embroidery and other forms of sewing. She was praised by the women for her tremendous talent with a needle and thread, but it raised no alarm. Her mother never spoke again of the *aes sidhe.* Helen carried the memory of Anne Connolly's fear, but she didn't share it, of course. She was an utterly practical modern American.

Years later, the Metropolitan Museum of Art opened its first restaurant and hired waitresses, Helen among them. She soon became famous throughout the building for making the most delicious, perfectly calibrated tea. One day, while serving tea to the Egyptology experts, she spotted a smudge on the side of a sarcophagus that everyone else seemed to have missed and couldn't resist removing it with her tea towel.

Her superiors were overjoyed with her deftness, her faultless instincts. It was a joke at first when museum scholars faced with cleaning or restoring challenges put in their request —"Send to the kitchen for Mrs. O'Neill!"—until, a few years having passed, she was made an employee of special status. There was no more "kitchen." Just "Send for Mrs. O'Neill." She couldn't be given the title of conservator, that was for people holding degrees from Harvard, Yale, or Princeton. Helen didn't care about titles. She was content handling the museum's possessions, taking pride in helping the sundry objects show their best features to the world. Museum experts trained her—they explained the critical importance of cleaning the acquisitions properly. The tiniest bits of dirt, grime, or any other foreign object could lead to serious damage, yet overzealous cleaning could damage something even more. Helen listened politely. She knew without being told what was required.

When a suit of Henry VIII's armor was being shown to Miss Belle da Costa Greene on behalf of Mr. Morgan as part of an upcoming exhibition, Helen made some final flicks on the breastplate to ensure the armor dazzled. "How extraordinary Mrs. O'Neill is," Belle said, a single woman's voice in the room. Except for Helen's, of course. But she rarely spoke to the men, just followed direction.

In a dizzyingly short amount of time, Helen found herself in the office of the museum's director to learn a whole new direction. "Mr. Morgan is the president of the Metropolitan Museum's board and our most important patron," Mr. Peterson said. Apparently, Belle had reported back on Helen O'Neill's extraordinariness, and the famously acquisitive millionaire had insisted on acquiring her.

Now, this wintry afternoon, in what must be the grandest

private library in America, Belle seemed happy as could be while watching Helen work. She didn't know it, but this provided Helen with a chance to get a closer look at her, too.

She's not as young as I first thought, but she really is lovely.

Belle's glowing skin was far different than Helen's ivory, faintly wrinkled complexion. It was the middle of the December, yet she looked as if she'd recently spent time in the sun. And those vivid green eyes. "She's from Portuguese nobility," someone told Helen her last day at the museum. That made her as exotic a creature to Helen as a tiger from the tropics.

"Do you have children, Mrs. O'Neill?"

Helen's fingers stilled for a fraction of a second on her brush. "No, Miss. Mr. O'Neill and I were married not even two years before he passed."

"Oh, how sad." A half minute passed before Belle said, "Of what did he die?"

She couldn't blame her. Hadn't Helen opened the door to such intrusions when she mentioned Stephen's delicate health? Without meeting Belle's gaze, she said, "My husband died in Cuba. Mr. O'Neill enlisted, became a soldier in the war with Spain in 1898. He contracted typhoid fever while serving his country."

"That's a terrible thing," said Belle.

"Thank you, Miss. It was."

There was a scaping sound as the chair across from Helen was pushed back. She looked up to see Belle on her feet, her face composed in an expression of chilly serenity. "That war had many complicated causes and outcomes," she said. "Carry on, Mrs. O'Neill."

Helen set down her brush, a flood of dismay coursing through her veins. There had been a feeling of harmony in the room, things were off to a fine start, she was deeply impressed with Miss Greene and wanted to impress *her*. Now it turned awkward.

After five o'clock, Belle reappeared to say that Helen could leave for the day. "I'm very glad you're here, Mrs. O'Neill," she said, her tone firm. Helen was certain her suspicion was correct, a coolness had sprung up between them because of her telling Belle about her husband's death. But Belle had wanted to hire her, and she seemed to need her. Moreover, she was a kind woman, Helen sensed. Hopefully, this would mend.

The security guard opened the bronze doors for Helen. Outside the sun had just set, dusk blending to darkness. To go from the dazzling bright rotunda to this made the entire street blur.

She regained her focus by the time she'd reached the sidewalk running along Thirty-Sixth Street. It was busier now, with horse-drawn carriages and motorcars rumbling by. As Helen walked toward Madison Avenue, she was struck by the golden circles emanating from the iron street lamps in front of the brownstones. Caught in the halos of light was a flurry of snowflakes. It must have just begun falling, for the sidewalk was merely damp, not white.

At the corner of Madison Avenue and Thirty-Sixth Street, a slip of a young woman stood with her hands resting on the low iron gate that ran along the sidewalk, facing the Morgan house. By the lamplight streaming across Madison Avenue, Helen could see that the girl wore a long, wide-skirted cream-colored dress, blue ribbons fluttering in the snowy breeze—but nothing else. No long coat, nor hat, nor gloves, nor sensible shoes. She had brown hair parted tightly in the center and fastened in two braids tucked at the base of her neck, but since the lamplight was behind her, not in front, Helen couldn't make out the expression on her face.

She must be freezing, Helen thought. *What on earth is the girl doing?*

Helen reached the corner, meaning she stood just three feet from the girl, who hadn't moved a bit but stood stock still, looking at the Morgan house. It was by no means certain anyone was home. Only two upstairs windows showed a light. There seemed no reason for her to stand watch, or whatever it was she was doing.

Although the way was clear for Helen to cross the street and continue down Madison Avenue to make her way to the train station, she hesitated. It was such a strange situation. Perhaps she should offer help.

For the first time, the girl moved, but it was only to turn her head a few inches toward Helen. Now her profile was visible: a long delicate nose, a slightly cleft chin. She seemed to realize Helen stood close by.

Is she waiting for me to say something? Helen wondered.

Feeling even more uncertain—and quite unnerved—Helen said nothing to the strange girl but turned away from her to cross the street. Moving quickly, not glancing back, she headed south on Madison Avenue.

CHAPTER 3

Saturdays in the Connolly house were frequently loud, but this one was especially frenetic because John Jr. planned a trip to the northern Bronx to pick out a small fir for the family Christmas tree, it being the second weekend in December, the traditional time for trees to appear in Irish homes.

"Aunt Helen, you must come with us—oh, you have to," said Rose. "And then help me pick out the ornaments."

Bending down to give her a hug to soften the blow, Helen said, "It'll be a pleasure to help you decorate, but I can't take the trip to the woods this afternoon."

"Not coming, Helen?" asked John Jr. sharply. "You always do, every year."

"We had the boy from St. Michael's, remember?" she prompted. "Sister Bernadette can see family after one o'clock."

And no one can quibble with that.

There was a fourth sibling in the family, an older daughter born Eileen and taking the name Bernadette when her life changed dramatically at age twenty-five. It was then that she took final vows at Corpus Christi Monastery, the oldest Dominican monastery of nuns in all of America, and it was to be found right here in Morrisania on Lafayette Avenue, a brisk walk from the Connolly house.

John Jr., Stephen, and Helen saw their sister just a handful of times a year. Corpus Christi was an enclosed order, which meant the nuns did not go out into the world, teaching or nursing. Their calling was fulfilled in cloistered seclusion. Sister Bernadette must obtain special permission to leave. Family could visit on certain Saturdays of the year but not without elaborate arrangements made ahead of time. Corpus Christi sent a Dominican friar with a message to the Connollys' place of worship, St. Michael's, and that church assigned an altar boy to run to their house relaying the approved date and time. Even had the Connollys owned a telephone, the monastery did not. This was the only way.

Naturally the Irish of Morrisania took tremendous pride in the Dominican monastery rising in their midst, and Eileen Connolly finding a place there as Sister Bernadette nudged the family higher in community status. Everyone agreed that the four had done well for themselves: a Dominican sister, a police sergeant, a teacher at a boys' academy, and then there was Helen, the diminutive widow who did some sort of work over the river, no one grasped what, but it was respectable.

"You must go to Corpus Christi if this is the day, to represent all of us," said Helen's sister-in-law, Siobhan, who helped to ease Rose's disappointment by popping a warm biscuit into her eager hands.

But John Jr. took a step closer to Helen and said, "The pine trees, that fresh country air, it'll do you good after sitting in a library all week. Have Stephen go this time."

"Stephen has his Music Society meeting, you know that. And I'll get loads of fresh air walking to Corpus Christi." She turned a bright smile on her oldest brother. "I'm fine."

"Humph," he grunted, pulling on his sideburns. Being a

good officer of the law, he could sniff out a liar in his home as well as in his precinct.

"You will be here when I put the candle in the window, won't you, Aunt Helen?" her niece persisted, as stubborn as her father. "It has to be the best red candle we have—you'll help me?"

"Oh, Rose, that's not until Christmas Eve! I will, pet."

Helen breathed a sigh of relief when John Jr. and his entire family finally trooped out the door in search of the perfect Christmas tree, carrying a basket of biscuits and jars of cider. She couldn't have put forth this false front much longer.

For the truth was, Helen's first week at Morgan's library left her in a troubled state. She badly needed to confide in someone, and yet the family members she lived with every day wouldn't understand. Helen wasn't certain that Sister Bernadette would either but turning to her older sister with her problems was still a habit of the heart, even if that sister left home many years ago.

Trudging along the slush-clogged Morrisania streets, Helen turned over in her mind what so unsettled her.

Why can't I put into words how I feel about what's happening at the library?

She couldn't blame Belle da Costa Greene. Any coolness between them on Monday afternoon was gone by Tuesday morning. She now grasped that Belle's moods shifted rapidly all day long, ricocheting from irritation with someone whom she was certain over-charged Mr. Morgan to exultation over a rare 15th century manuscript. Helen had even witnessed her in full flirtation: When complimented by a library guest for the fashionable gown she wore, Belle tossed her head and said, "I may be a librarian, but that doesn't mean I have to dress like one!"

Helen was more impressed by Belle da Costa Greene every day. No matter her flashes of humor, she took her position extremely seriously. To her, the money of J. P. Morgan could not be squandered, never mind his legendary wealth. She went about her tasks with diligence, discretion, and concentration, aided by specially designed furniture. The catalog case had a revolving upper portion, and her chair revolved too. She had the use of two small writing tables with secrets doors equipped with spring pushes. No one without knowledge of the position of the pushes could open anything.

Yet a clear source of worry for Belle was J. P. Morgan's continued presence in Washington, D.C. Gradually, Helen perceived it wasn't that Belle missed his physical presence but that something unpleasant was taking place in Washington. "Oh, how can they be so unfair to him?" Belle said while speaking on the telephone with real anguish. "They blame him for everything. Do you know I read in an awful newspaper he was behind the sinking of the *Titanic*!"

But the reality of Helen's new position was that she didn't have a lot to do with Belle or any other person. Her work assignments were set in the morning. Hours passed by when she didn't catch a glimpse of her employer—after all, she worked in the main library and Belle mostly kept to her office. The various assistants and guards passed in and out of the room, performing duties without speaking to Helen, sometimes not even glancing in her direction. A few times a day someone pulled the lever and ascended one of the two hidden staircases.

It all made her realize how accustomed she'd become to not only the large size but also the high spirits of the staff at the Metropolitan Museum of Art. Working in their midst, she'd often been party to the happy frenzy, to their congratulating one another over the arrival of a new painting or tomb. Their attitude even on occasion turned to gloating, such as remarking —with a wink and a smile—on the misfortune of the poor nobles in England, those dukes, earls, and lords, at being forced to part with their most beloved paintings due to the new British tax laws. In a steady exodus, Old Master paintings sailed across the Atlantic to take their places on the Metropolitan's lofty walls.

In the vast, ornate, silent Morgan library, no one gloated. It wasn't a grim work atmosphere by any means but sitting at her table, dusting and cleaning and repairing, Helen was sometimes overcome by a sense of ... dread. That was the only word for it. Time and again, she caught herself holding her breath and clenching her fingers, but there was absolutely no reason for it. She struggled to shake off the nagging feeling that something was about to happen to her, any minute. More than that. A nasty surprise was hovering around the corner.

The surprise never comes, so why I am so worried?

Lord, what a toll it took. Helen felt wary even now, walking a street lined with grocers and butchers and stationers and pubs, passing people she'd known for years. A few waved at Helen. The Irish were one part of the community; the Germans had made homes here first. In the last several years, Italian families settled in Morrisania too. The opening of the subway not only made it easier for Helen and others to go to Manhattan but also led new people to the Bronx.

She was in the heart of her community, on the way to visit the sister she loved with all her heart. What was so wrong?

She brightened at the sight of Corpus Christi Monastery off Lafayette Road and let herself in through the front gate. As she walked up the path, its church and chapel, living quarters, kitchens, grounds, and garden spread out before her, covering many acres.

Outsiders could enter the chapel. Anyone was welcome to worship there among the nuns and friars. No Mass was being held at present; just a few finding a place to pray, hunched over while murmuring pleas and clutching their Rosary beads.

Helen quickly made her way to the rack placed before the statue of the Virgin Mary; it held a great many tall, slender white candles, half of them lit. She selected an unlit taper, moved its tip to one that was flickering to ignite it, and then carefully found the right place for her candle. For a few seconds a profound tenderness glowed, softening Helen's sharp features. The light flickering in her blue eyes, she whispered a prayer. With a sigh and a final wistful glance at her busy little candle, she turned away.

It was time for Sister Bernadette.

CHAPTER 4

The elderly woman stationed inside the adjoining office smiled at Helen's arrival. A heavy set of keys in her hand, she tottered to the other door and unlocked it. This was where families met with the sisters. Seeing Sister Bernadette inside the windowless room, wearing her black and white habit, made Helen's face erupt into a joyous smile.

They couldn't hug each other because of the divider, a low wooden barrier meant to maintain the proper distance between the two worlds. As was their custom, the siblings grabbed each other's forearms in a sort of exaggerated handshake.

Helen handed over the barrier her usual gift, a canister of shortbread cookies, and settled into the hard-backed chair pulled out for her.

"Yum, yum," said Bernadette, prying the lid off the cannister.

When she was still Eileen Connolly, the big-boned, blonde, blue-eyed oldest daughter of the family was known for her love of fun, relishing practical jokes and devouring the comic strips. She was the most popular girl in her classes, worshipped by friends. It was a shock to the school as well as to her family when Eileen announced her calling, her intention to take vows and seal herself away from the outside world. First she was a novice, serving for years, then a full-fledged nun. Her family worried that a life revolving around prayer might suppress her spirits. But Sister Bernadette smiled and joked in the monastery meeting room just as Eileen once did in the family parlor.

Peering at her over a shortbread cookie, Sister Bernadette said, "You look so tired, is J. P. Morgan working you too hard, love?"

"It's hardly difficult work," shrugged Helen. "And I've never met the man, he hasn't shown himself in the library yet."

"I would say not, seeing that he's in Washington, D.C., being scolded by the senators who blame him for all our country's ills," said Sister Bernadette.

"I can't believe you know this!"

"I can't believe you *don't*—and you under the man's roof," Sister Bernadette said with a laugh, adding that her source was two friars discussing news of the hearing in Washington, D.C. "Tell me what it's really like to work there."

Rather than seizing this opening to explain the apprehension, Helen found herself listing the highlights of J. P. Morgan's manuscript collection—Dickens's original *A Christmas Carol*, the sole surviving manuscript of John Milton's *Paradise Lost*, Henry David Thoreau's journals, Thomas Jefferson's letters to his daughter Martha, letters of Jane Austen, Charlotte Brontë, Abraham Lincoln...the famous names tumbled out of her mouth, on and on, until Sister Bernadette held up her hand like a referee pleading for a time out.

"And that's only a part of the library," Helen mumbled, her voice trailing away. "Then there are the illuminated manuscripts."

Sister Bernadette flicked a cookie crumb off her brilliant white habit. "If you wanted to, could you return to the other place, the Metropolitan Museum of Art?"

Helen sat back in her chair, astounded. "Why would I? It'd be an insult to Miss Greene after all the trouble she's taken to make a place for me. Mr. Morgan is the most important art collector in the whole city. The museum would be mortified if I slunk away, not welcome me with open arms."

Sister Bernadette said nothing, her blue eyes studying her sister, much as John Jr. had earlier in the day.

"Why would you even ask me that?" Helen asked, though it came out as more like a plea.

"It was merely a question. We Dominicans are famous for posing questions."

"Excuse me, but this isn't a class on St. Thomas Aquinas," said Helen, upset.

To that, no response was made, and a full minute of silence crawled by, until Helen said, "There's nothing wrong with the library, but I have noticed something odd outside the library. Or someone, to be specific."

With that, Helen felt a cold thrill of excitement. She hadn't intended to speak of this, but the words were out, there was no going back.

What a relief it will be to unburden myself.

"Please share with me what troubles you," her sister said encouragingly.

Helen explained what she'd seen that first evening: the young girl with sleek brown hair who stood outside the Morgan home, staring up at the windows with such concentration, not at all dressed for the cold of December yet seeming not to feel it.

"Oh, the rich aren't always practical," Sister Bernadette said. "She might have had a carriage waiting and was looking for a friend. Mr. Morgan perhaps has daughters she expected to meet?"

"Perhaps," said Helen, remembering the photograph of the daughters in Belle's office. They were in their thirties or forties.

And she was certain that a well-bred young girl would not stand on a cold street looking at a window but send in her servant or carriage driver to make inquiries while she remained in the carriage. Sister Bernadette had not mingled with the upper class before she sealed herself away in the monastery. And Helen had not yet told her everything.

She said, hesitantly, "The second time I saw the girl outside was a little different."

"The same girl?"

"On Thursday, after I left the library, she was on the block again, not in the same place but farther up, halfway between Thirty-Sixth Street and Thirty-Seventh Street. I saw her as I walked toward Madison Avenue, among all the others on the sidewalk. There were quite a few of them, sometimes there are people on Madison and other times it's practically deserted." Helen paused to gather her recollection in all its specifics. "I could tell, with the lamplights glowing across the street, that she wore the same dress as before—sort of flowing and light in color with blue ribbons—and still without a cloak or coat. She was standing still, looking up at Mr. Morgan's house. I made it to the corner, and I admit I stood there, watching her, trying to puzzle her out."

Sitting there in the safety of a Dominican monastery, Helen felt moisture gather in her palms, a certain clamminess, as she pushed on with the story.

"Just at that moment, with me staring at her, she turned toward me and started walking to the corner, right toward where I was standing, and I could see the expression of her face. She was glad—she was glad to see me! As if we knew each other. I have never seen this girl before, not before this past week. But I was curious, so I stayed put, though I wasn't completely happy to be singled out by a stranger."

Not "completely happy"? She'd been in an agony of indecision, not knowing if she should wait for this girl to reach her spot or turn and run across the street to get away from her.

Sister Bernadette said, "What happened when she approached you—what did she say?"

"Nothing. Because she didn't reach the corner. Two men pushed past me, I was in their way I suppose, and they walked up Madison in the path of where she would have had to walk, and when they'd made it a ways, I couldn't see her any longer."

"Where did she go?"

"I don't know. I think she must have changed her mind and turned around and walked in the same direction as the men, ahead of them, and I couldn't see her anymore. I didn't go searching. I walked to Pennsylvania Station to come home."

Helen rubbed her damp palms on her skirt and waited for her sister's response.

Sister Bernadette fiddled with the cookie cannister before saying, "Did the girl seem angry at all, any malicious intent?"

She shook her head.

"Well, then, I'm not sure why you're in a tizzy over this, Helen. It was dark, she mistook you for someone else, and the closer she got, she realized her mistake and didn't say anything to you but turned back. Seems reasonable."

"It isn't reasonable—there's nothing *reasonable* about her. To wear the exact same dress three days apart while lingering at night on Madison Avenue?"

Sister Bernadette tried on a smile. "It may have escaped your notice, but I wear similar clothing every day."

With that, Helen's body tensed in frustration.

How awful to leave Corpus Christi without making myself understood.

She had no choice but to push forward—again—to try to explain. "She looked at me and even from half a block, I could feel this strange sort of ... recognition. It was important to her, I was important to her. And no one ever notices me on the street or thinks me of any importance. I'm practically invisible."

With that, Sister Bernadette's eyes were full of concern, and she spoke soothingly to Helen of how much everyone cared for her, that she was anything but invisible. The more she tried to comfort her younger sister, the more wretched Helen felt.

The conversation shifted to the others in the family—how was Stephen's health? Still suffering from headaches? And was John Jr.'s second oldest child doing any better in school? How were plans for Rose's First Communion? To Helen, growing angry, these were just signposts on a road rarely traveled, items of conversation to prove she cared about the other Connollys.

But does she really?

"We don't have too much time left together," said Sister Bernadette. "I thought I should share some news pertaining to me. I am to serve as the new novice mistress here, helping the young newcomers to adjust and to make sure of their vocations."

Something inside Helen snapped.

Gripped the narrow wooden tabletop of the divider, Helen said, her eyes narrowed, "Oh, yes, you'll help them, won't you? But where were you when I needed you?"

Her sister recoiled. "Helen—Helen—I can't believe you'd say that to me."

"Right. Who'd ever criticize the high and mighty Sister Bernadette? But you know what you did to me—what you did to Sean!" Her voice broke on the name of her husband.

"Oh, what do you mean, what are you talking about?" pleaded Sister Bernadette, her hands reaching out over the divider as if she were trying to grab hold of Helen.

"He liked you so much! More than anyone else in the family. He looked up to you as if you were sitting on the cloud next to God. You know that—you liked it well enough. But when I asked you for help after he died? What a different story!"

Tears brimmed in Sister Bernadette's eyes. "Helen, Helen, you know the rules of the Dominican Order. There was nothing I could do. I told you, nothing. It was impossible."

Helen stumbled to her feet. "Forget it, what does it matter to you? Go to your novices. Don't let me delay you."

Sister Bernadette rose, too, although the divider meant she could not come over to Helen's side of the room. "It was fourteen years ago, Helen," she said, tears rolling down her cheeks.

Helen stalked to the door, only turning to spit out the words, "Goodbye, *Eileen!*"

She made her way out of the monastery, using her handkerchief to blow her nose in the hallway as if she had a cold to hide her own tears. Halfway down the path that led to the road, however, Helen turned around, her face grim, and marched around the far side of the building, toward an arch. She moved quickly, hoping no one would stop her from reaching her destination. But on a cold day such as this, none of the nuns, friars, or lay monastics worked outside that she could see.

Helen passed under the arch, entering the cemetery of Corpus Christi, the tombstones neatly ordered in a giant square, about one-third of the stones hung with wreaths or sporting dried-up flowers in vases placed carefully alongside.

Her heart pounding in her chest like a terrible drum, Helen stumbled toward the left perimeter of the cemetery. A tall stone angel rose there, between two maple trees with leaves long ago fallen. She was a lovely angel—the sculptor had given her a serene wide brow and a bow-shaped mouth.

Sister Bernadette was right about one thing, it was fourteen years ago. And a year earlier than that, when Sean and Helen, after a tour of the grounds on a July afternoon, lingered by the statue of the angel while the young nun chatted with the cemetery keeper under the arch.

As if it were yesterday, Helen could see her husband, tall and broad-shouldered, a hat perched on his head, push back a strand of brown hair so he could better see the stone angel.

"Wouldn't that be peaceful—resting for eternity with an angel like her watching over me?" he said thoughtfully.

"You, peaceful?" said Helen, poking him. "That I'd like to see."

"I could rest nice and peaceful here," he said, sweeping his arm across the cemetery. "You'll see to it, Helen?"

"Bad luck to speak of that," she insisted. "Say a prayer, quickly."

"We'll say one together," he said, putting his arm around her. "But I like the thought of you bringing our children and our little grandbabies here to visit me."

A cold wind whistled through the cemetery, jolting Helen back to the present. No grave for Sean here. The sun was sinking lower in the sky. Twilight would darken the cemetery and barren garden before too long. Back at home, the others would soon expect her. Helen walked up the path to Lafayette Road, her head bowed in misery. Behind her the voices of the nuns could be heard through the wall, chanting their prayers.

CHAPTER 5

The quarrel with her sister left Helen both angry and ashamed —and, most of all, utterly drained. By the time she had made it home, John Jr.'s family was caught up in a frenzy of tree decorating. Helen managed to make it through the evening by force of will, and with two cups of coffee. She refused to disappoint her niece Rose, who was shrieking with joy at the sight of the most cherished family ornaments removed from their tissue-lined boxes.

It was not just her affection for Rose that made her want to do this. Dressing the tree had always pleased Helen, as in a fashion it revealed through ornaments how far the family had come. The two most fragile had come the farthest—in more ways than one. Stored in a box that made the trip to America with their mother Anne Connolly, then Anne Devlin, were two fragile ornaments with centers in the shapes of Celtic knots, interlinking circles.

Looking at the Celtic knots makes me feel a bit better, no matter what else is happening in my life.

The sight of them didn't make *everyone* happy. "Are these Christian symbols?" her sister-in-law once asked doubtfully. Perhaps she disliked the reminder that her late mother-in-law might have held beliefs one might describe as pre-Christian, which was a nice way of saying pagan. "My husband's family was lace-curtain Irish, not shanty Irish," Siobhan said at a family wedding within hearing of Stephen, who told Helen of it with an eye roll. Brother and sister knew their family roots and accepted them. John Connolly Sr. had liked to tease his wife that the first time she put on shoes was when she left for the boat to America.

Stephen absented himself from the day's tree-decorating festivities without anyone complaining about it. They all knew that his Music Society meetings meant the world to him, giving him a chance to debate opera with friends. Wagner or Strauss? Such debates could rage for hours. Stephen didn't make it home until after supper, his breath smelling of brandy. He paid the obligatory compliments to everyone over the tree's glory, his natural facility with words glossing over a fundamental indifference.

"And how did you find the blessed Sister Bernadette today?" he asked Helen with the faintly ironic tone that his older sister inspired.

"She's well," Helen said shortly and then announced she would be going upstairs early because of a headache. Walking up the steps, she could feel the eyes of her family upon her. They knew something was wrong.

Helen used the excuse of a lingering headache to skip church Sunday and take dinner on a tray in her room as well.

I must gather all my strength to face Morgan's library on Monday.

Thankfully, in the cold light of morning, when the Morgan house and the man's library rose before her on Madison Avenue, Helen felt no fear. All seemed normal. Motorcars rumbled past; people waited to dart across the street. On the block itself, a string of men wearing serious hats and outercoats strode down the sidewalk, their heads bowed against the stiff winter wind pouring off the East River. There was no sign of the girl, and Helen felt suddenly ridiculous for her preoccupation. What had come over her? She lost her temper and hurled terrible accusations at her sister that she now wished she could take back.

Once inside the library, engulfed by marble and stone and oil paint, Helen experienced a surge of pride that she was employed in a place of such beauty. She took her place at the worktable in the vast main library, ready to start work. Minutes later, *click-click-click* announced Belle da Costa Greene coming across the rotunda. Then the woman appeared, holding something before her as if she led a solemn procession, though no one followed.

"Mrs. O'Neill, you passed with such flying colors last week —not that I expected anything less—that today I would like you to examine one of the library's treasures," said Belle. "This is Mr. Morgan's pride and joy."

With great care, Belle placed before her a large book, wrapped in softest fabric. It had a cover that shimmered and dazzled: gold, pearls, and emeralds danced among the more staid sculpted figures, the dominant one of Christ on the Cross, his arms outstretched.

"This, what you see before you, are the Lindau Gospels." Belle's voice trembled with excitement. "We believe the covers and the manuscript pages date from slightly different periods, but it was all created in the Carolingian Period, which leads us to Emperor Charlemagne. Inside are the four gospels and other religious material. But it's the covers that make this a masterpiece. Our consulting scholars' best guess is that the front cover you see before you was crafted in the ninth century in the Abbey of Lindau in Germany, hence the name. Isn't it breathtaking?"

"It is, Miss," murmured Helen, though at that moment it wasn't a pleasurable sensation at all.

I can't draw breath—the dread is returning.

"You can really feel the Carolingians' determination while looking at this cover," continued Belle, not noticing Helen's discomfort. "They *would* bring order and knowledge to this new empire through faith, through the Gospels. We know Charlemagne was a warlord, there's no question. He might even be considered a mass murderer by today's standards, if you look at what he did to carve out his empire. Utterly ruthless. But then—to commission this, what you see before you. Amazing. The expense of the jeweled cover and the hard work, all those monks bent over writing the script for years and years."

Helen nodded, unable to trust herself to speak for the feeling of being overwhelmed.

Belle put something else on Helen's worktable, a notebook and pencil. "Let's try something a little different, shall we? Instead of you touching the Lindau Gospels right away, please examine the covers and make notes of what you'd recommend first? I will go over your notes with my consultant on manuscript restoring, and then you can proceed. I'm sure everything you wish to do will be in order, but this extra step is necessary, given the value of Mr. Morgan's acquisition. He paid a whole fifty thousand dollars for this."

Staring down at the shimmering metalwork cover, Helen was seized by a wild impulse to stand up and run out the door. But the tough, resilient core that pulsed within Helen O'Neill extinguished that impulse.

I must find a way to perform the tasks I've been hired to do.

After Belle returned to her office, Helen took pencil in hand. Seeking some sort of help, some guidance, she looked up—up at the ceiling of the main library. Staring back at her was a figure of a man sitting on a chair that rested on a cloud, gesturing kindly to another man kneeling before him. How comforting to have such holy figures looking down. This must be Our Lord, his archangels, and some of the saints.

She took a deep breath and scrutinized the cover. This wasn't how she worked. Helen didn't proceed from written instructions. Whenever she approached a statue, a painting, or a manuscript, it seemed to speak to her, to mysteriously invite her touch. But having no choice, she proceeded as told to by Belle. With her perfect eyesight, she took in the details of the pearls and emeralds and, most of all, the figure of Christ. This body of the Savior showed less abject suffering than what she usually observed in medieval paintings and books. Just miniscule pools of blood sculpted below his pierced palms.

Going slowly, taking deep breaths, gazing up at the ceiling frescoes, Helen moved forward, scribbling notes in her book every few minutes. The dread never left, it caught her breath and nipped at her thoughts, but she was able to keep the feeling at bay enough to write some notes.

When next Belle stopped by, the head librarian smiled at the sight of some writing. "Fine work, Mrs. O'Neill, fine work." Belle glanced around the room and said, "You take inspiration from these surroundings, I take it."

"Oh, yes," answered Helen, pleased that Belle understood. "May I inquire, is Mr. Morgan a religious man?"

"I'll say he is. A devout Episcopalian. His Connecticut grandfather gave quite fiery sermons, he once mentioned. He's a founding member of the Church Club of New York."

So the man's a Protestant? Aloud, she said, "He does seem appreciative of the holy saints."

"Saints?" Belle's eyebrows scrunched in confusion. "Yes, I suppose so. Oh. Wait. Do you mean *them?*" She pointed skyward. "No saints up there. Those are his zodiac frescoes, Mrs. O'Neill. Each of the paintings represents a different astrological sign."

Now Helen was not just surprised but dumbfounded. She'd been taught that following the constellations in the sky, believing that the sun and stars could guide human behavior, was foolish. Some would even say sinful. To believe in the Zodiac was to worship dark forces perhaps.

Catching something of her reaction, Belle said quickly, "But Mr. Morgan has collected many books and paintings of a Christian nature as well as those revolving around astrological and classical subjects. I mean you've been studying the Landau Gospels all morning." She clapped her hands lightly. "This is all my fault. I must apologize for not giving you a 'tour,' so to speak, of our wonderful ceiling art."

With that, she pulled Helen to her feet and took her around the room, pointing at the various figures above that represented the Zodiac, each of them grouped with their ruling deities from the Roman calendar. It turned out Helen had mistaken the water carrier Aquarius next to Neptune for God and one of his archangels. "Mr. Morgan first took the idea, I think, from his monthly dinners with the other members of the Zodiac Club at Delmonico's."

"A Zodiac Club?" Helen could not suppress her astonishment.

Belle shrugged and smiled. "Yes, there are never more or less than twelve members. Mr. Morgan is Brother Libra, he told me once, though outsiders are not meant to know such details. These Zodiac figures are not in the correct chronological order and he simply won't tell me why. There is a reason. Yes, he draws ideas and inspirations from all sorts of places, Mrs. O'Neill. He's even met with clairvoyants and psychics."

After finishing her astrological briefing, Belle pointed out the theme of another part of the ceiling, the muses along with their companion luminaries: Dante, Socrates, Herodotus. Helen's head swam, but Belle was far from finished. She guided her employee out into the rotunda to continue her "ceiling tour." She was in the middle of explaining one of three groupings when Helen felt a strange prickling up her arms and a tightening of her throat. In a group of epic poets of antiquity, a young man with dark hair and a bare shoulder sat on a step, holding a musical instrument.

That's just the way he'd tilt his head, listening when sitting in a chair.

"Is there something wrong, Mrs. O'Neill?" Helen heard the voice as if from afar.

Her ordinarily high-pitched voice gone deep and harsh, Helen asked, "The man with the harp, who is he?"

"Ah, that's Orpheus."

The name meant nothing to Helen. She had not asked for the stories behind any other person of myth or legend, but about this person painted far above her head, she had to know more. "Could you tell me the story of Orpheus?"

"Oh, let me see. The greatest musician of them all, either gods or mortals. The son of Apollo and the muse Calliope. He loved his wife—I can't recall her name—and when she died young, he traveled to the underworld to try to persuade Hades and Persephone to let him have his wife back. Her persuaded them to release her, but the condition was, when the two of them walked out of the underworld, Orpheus must promise to never look back, look back at his wife walking right behind him. Of course he did—you know how these stories go—and just before they had emerged into the daylight, he looked back and his wife vanished forever in a puff."

Peering at her more closely, Belle said, "Do you need to sit down? A glass of water?"

"No—no, I'm fine," stammered Helen. "I will be getting back to my work now."

The afternoon was then lost to serious work. For the first time in her life, Helen was unable to push down her worries or fears and get on with it. The cover of the Lindau Gospels sat there, mute to Helen in all its bejeweled glory. A hundred urgent memories crowded her head instead.

Sean, Sean, it's you in the ceiling—it could be you.

Light still filtered through the high windows in the room when Belle returned, saying that because the afternoon's snowfall threatened to become a blizzard, it might be best for Helen to depart early.

"And you did look a bit peaked earlier," said Belle quietly. "I wouldn't want you to be up against it with the weather."

What a kind woman she is.

Although she was never a shirker for work—no Connolly ever was—Helen welcomed an end to this day. She gathered her things from the cloakroom, keeping her line of sight low. She wasn't ready to look once more at the dark-haired man who resembled her dead husband.

Outside, a steady flurry of snow slanted down on streets already blanketed white. It was late afternoon, sunset maybe an hour away. Helen pulled her scarf tighter around her throat and glanced down, careful to watch where she stepped. A fall on the sidewalk here, in front of the library, promised to be not just painful but embarrassing.

A man hurried past her on the sidewalk clutching his business satchel. People were trying to reach their destinations as quickly as they could. Helen looked ahead to the corner of Thirty-Sixth Street and Madison Avenue, where she always made her turn, to see if the gathering snow would present difficulties.

Helen came to a halt so sudden that her shoes slipped and skidded on the sidewalk.

This cannot be happening—not now, not today.

Walking straight toward Helen, with no one between them at all, was the girl in the long cream-colored dress.

CHAPTER 6

In the light of day, two things became apparent. One was the type of dress the girl wore was unlike any of the dresses Helen had seen on girls from fine New York families. It was cinched tight in the waist—revealing that she was not just slender but extremely thin—and below that the dress extended and curved like a bell. The blue ribbons Helen noticed before were tacked to the sides of her bodice, which was tightly buttoned up to the base of her throat. It was a dress for a modest, retiring young female.

And for the first time Helen could make out the girl's features. She was not a beauty—she was more than that. Hers was a face of distinction and intelligence and kindness, a smile on her lips. But there was something else. Helen detected shadows under her eyes and a hollowness under her cheeks. Yet she smiled with purpose, a gathering determination even.

Helen's heart pumped in her chest, for today, more than ever, it seemed madness for someone who didn't look at all strong to wear a light dress—made of cotton or muslin—in conditions such as these. In this blizzard, how could the snow fail to accumulate on her hair, drawn back in two coils? But it gleamed dark brown without a snowflake on top.

Such an old-fashioned way to style your hair.

A man, speeding up, veering closer to the street, passed the girl on her right without a second glance in her direction, which Helen found surprising. Surely others must find her strange? This wasn't night-time, when her appearance was cloaked in darkness and shadows, illuminated only by the light of the streetlamps. This was broad daylight.

The girl was no more than three feet from Helen now. She lifted her hand in a wave, as if delighted. There was absolutely no question that she sought out Helen specifically. Well, at least she'd finally find out what the girl had to say. Though part of her was deeply unnerved, Helen wanted to have the matter dealt with.

This has gone on long enough.

Someone tugged on Helen's arm. "Are you quite all right, Mrs. O'Neill?" asked the guard with the black moustache, the same one who'd opened the door to Helen her first morning at the library. His name was Mr. Lawrence. Apparently he'd been let go early as well.

"Yes, I'm fine," said Helen, turning to him.

"Then pardon me for asking, but why are you just standing on the street here? Shouldn't you be heading to your home? I understand that you live fairly far, in the Bronx. It's not a time to linger."

Not knowing how else to explain herself, Helen said, "I'm conversing with this young lady," half-pointing at her.

"Who?" he asked, squinting.

Helen turned back toward the girl, and a gasp escaped her. No one stood there. Ten feet farther up, a trio of men hurried toward Helen and Mr. Lawrence on the sidewalk, the snow coming down harder. Helen craned her neck to look up and down and across Thirty-Sixth Street. The girl had somehow slipped away, though it seemed impossible.

Mr. Lawrence insisted on escorting Helen to Pennsylvania

Station. Words failed her during the entire walk; fortunately, Mr. Lawrence was not one for chatter either, especially with snow stinging their faces.

By the time she'd reached the Connolly house by train, trolley car, and on foot, Helen had convinced herself that the girl must have been overcome by shyness when Mr. Lawrence tugged on Helen's arm and darted away. Wearing a light-colored dress in the snow, she'd be hard to spot. There was no other explanation.

The fact that the man passing by hadn't seemed to see the girl—and Mr. Lawrence definitely hadn't seen her at all—filled Helen with frustration. At this point, she very much wanted to discuss the matter with someone. But as she'd learned after talking to her sister, it was hard to convey in words just what was so deeply strange about encountering a well-dressed young girl who, after all, never did anything "wrong." Whenever she neared Helen, she was amiable and genteel.

The next two days offered a reprieve in one regard—no more sighting of the girl, day or night, near or far. Yet Helen was far from serene. She had two sources of grief: First was the constant reminder of her husband in the Orpheus of the rotunda ceiling. When she tried to avoid looking up, that was no good. She could almost hear Sean laughingly reproach her: "Are you too busy, Helen, to give your husband the time of day?" But whenever she did steal a glance upward, it sent a shiver of sad longing through her. All these years later, she ached to feel Sean toss his arm around her shoulder, pulling her in for a quick kiss. She ached for other things as well.

The second source of grief was the Landau Gospels. The more Helen tried to complete her work assignment the way Belle wanted it done, the more impossible that became. Whether it was throwing Jacks, embroidering lace collars, making tea, or cleaning valuable art and artifacts, Helen never deliberated or calculated in her approach. When her fingers reached toward any object, the next action taken—the touching —occurred before she could articulate it, much less plan it.

With her own very particular and inexplicable way of doing things barred, Helen found herself brooding over the Gospels themselves. She didn't think about Charlemagne and his brutal conquest, nor the holy story of Jesus relayed in the Gospels. She found herself wondering about the lives of the monks who created this over a millennium ago. While still at the Metropolitan Museum of Art, she had assisted on a project restoring an illuminated manuscript from the medieval period. One day the curator found a tiny scribble in the margin made by a monk. What theological pondering was this? They were all very excited. With a magnifying glass, the curator translated it for everyone: "While I wrote I froze, and what I could not write by the beam of the sun I finished by candlelight." Amid the laughter, that same curator frowned, saying he had read that the monks suffering crippling neck and back pain and went blind after years of such labor. Surveying the pages of perfect script on delicate pages, Helen felt waves of compassion for the scribes' suffering.

What on earth is the matter with me?

Morbid musings had no business here. At the Metropolitan Museum of Art, the others praised Helen's sensible approach to objects that in other people's hands caused melancholic if not ghoulish ponderings. How many sarcophaguses had she brushed! The same curator who translated the monk's lament told her that the word *sarcophagus* derived from the phrase "flesh eating stone." She shrugged it all off.

If no inner strength were to be found, Helen yearned to turn somewhere outside herself for comfort. The time was over for drawing spiritual strength from her exquisite surroundings, however. Now that she knew this wasn't God and his archangels looking down but Zodiac signs paired with figures from Greek mythology, Helen felt anything but protected. With her excellent eyesight, she detected that one of the Zodiac groupings even included a man holding the severed head of a woman with coils of hair. How ghastly.

Whenever Belle da Costa Greene stopped by Helen's worktable and glanced at the page of tentative suggestions on the Lindau Gospels, her eyebrows dented in elegant bafflement. Helen's employer was too polite to voice disappointment—for the time being. The amorphous dread consuming Helen could become real and specific: Belle da Costa Greene's regret at hiring her.

But on Thursday of that week the Morgan Library transformed itself in such a dramatic fashion that Helen O'Neill's faltering at her tasks was a secondary matter. The man himself, John Pierpont Morgan, was through with Washington, D.C., and roaring back to New York. He just might arrive by supper time.

Belle da Costa Greene was in a tizzy, to quote Sister Bernadette. She darted here and there, writing down all sorts of information for the necessary reports to Mr. Morgan. Her assistants scrambled to comply with all requests, while the guards strode about with new energy too. Helen overheard them talking about bringing up something from "the tunnel." She hadn't known one existed.

The biggest clue of all to J. P. Morgan's imminent arrival was the opening of his study. How strange to have those tall doors flung open. Helen wasn't sure what she expected of the study of New York's titan of finance except for one thing: The room couldn't possibly have red walls. Yet that is exactly what jumped out at her when she peered inside. The walls of the room were covered with red damask silk. It pulsed and glowed behind the paintings and furniture. A massive desk dominated the far side of the room. Bronze dogs guarded each side of the briskly roaring fireplace, with a framed portrait of Mr. Morgan mounted above. Of course the windows were exceptional:

Stained glass panels that would have looked at home in a French cathedral when the first King Louis ruled his land.

While gaping, she heard Belle da Costa Greene's heels on the marble floor. She came to stand at Helen's side, smiling as if she couldn't blame anyone for being drawn to the doorway. "What a handsome room, wouldn't you say, Mrs. O'Neill? It's quite a historic one, too. I must tell you that in 1907, Mr. Morgan locked the leaders of finance in New York in this very study while he played solitaire in the library. He wouldn't let them out until they'd come to agreement over how the nation would restructure and pull itself out of a panic."

"Oh, my, that is something," Helen said. Morgan really did hold the fate of America in his hands.

Belle said gently, "You won't ever have reason to be in here, but it's fine to look for now."

Embarrassed, Helen retreated to her worktable.

When she left for the day on Thursday, the man himself had not yet arrived. But it was clear he was imminent, for his house brimmed with electric light and candlelight and noise, the busy humming of many voices. This would be the time for someone who knew the family to appear, seeking entry, but there was no sign of the ethereal girl on Madison Avenue or Thirty-Sixth Street.

It was Friday, December 20, that the man who built himself a private library to the specifications of a scholar potentate and filled it with treasure returned. Now there were guards outside the tall brass doors as well as inside, strolling the rotunda.

Her stomach fluttering, Helen put her things away in the cloakroom. The door to Mr. Morgan's study was ajar. Male voices murmured inside. The strongest clue to a new presence was smell: a whiff that was like bitter grass and rich, rain-soaked earth filled the rotunda. She knew what a cigar smelled like but had never inhaled one like this.

Helen opened her notebook, determined that this would be

the day she'd break through her hesitancies and make progress with the Lindau Gospels. And the morning did yield a new method for her. She cast back in her mind to occasions when she'd taken care of similar surfaces and objects and wrote down her approach in each of those cases. This could be the way forward.

Several hours later, the noise level tripled. Mr. Morgan and his companions in the study had entered the rotunda. A moment after that, the doorway filled with the tall, broad presence of J. P. Morgan, casting his eyes around the room until they settled on Helen O'Neill, frozen in her chair. The famously fierce black-eyed stare raked over her small frame.

Oh, but he's so very old.

White haired and wrinkled with yes, a mottled red drooping nose. The dominant emotion that she picked up on though was weariness. It rolled across the room with the same strength as his cigar smoke. Unsure what to do, Helen pushed back her chair, preparing to stand and introduce herself. But Mr. Morgan had already turned away. "To Keens, gentlemen," he said, his voice gruff. Doors opened and slammed shut, as Mr. Morgan and company strode a few blocks over for their lunch of thick steaks.

Helen consumed her own sack lunch of dark brown bread and liverwurst purchased at the German delicatessen in Morrisania, thinking over her first glimpse of the man in the flesh. He was outwardly commanding but a mortal man after all; surrounding himself with timeless classics of art and literature couldn't change that.

She'd been back at her desk for more than an hour when Mr. Morgan returned, this time making his way to the study directly. She heard the heavy doors boom shut. Feeling inspired by the presence of the man responsible for her employment, Helen dedicated yet more energy to her work.

As she made a note about one of the figures lamenting the

Crucifixion on the lower half of the cover, Helen heard a faint noise, coming from above and to the right. It was like a book being pulled from its place on a higher-level balcony, yet no one had clicked open a staircase. She looked up, half-turning in her chair.

"No!"

The word flew from her lips as she locked eyes with the young brown-haired girl, standing in front of books shelved on the highest balcony. She was inside J. P. Morgan's private library —inside the room where Helen worked. She didn't radiate delight this time. Her expression was utterly serious, as if Helen were at fault and she'd come to correct her.

Helen sprang to her feet. The guards were just outside, Belle da Costa Greene a moment away. This time she would find another person to witness the presence of the girl—she couldn't slip away in the snow—and get some answers.

But what if she *did* get away in the time it took Helen to summon someone else? There were two hidden staircases to the bookshelves. She could find a way to hide herself.

I'm going straight up there to bring you back down!

It was appalling that she'd found a way inside, that the girl had wormed her way into a place she had no business being. Miss Greene would be aghast.

Helen ran to the corner of the quadrangle. This was the entranceway people used, and where she had stood as she watched Belle pull the necessary lever. Helen groped for the lever, but there were only books on the shelf. Frantic, she scanned the next highest shelf, and spotted it. Helen pulled the lever down and stepped back as the entrance to the stairs swung open.

Up she went, circling around on the steps, and with each one she grew angrier. Why was this girl persisting in trying to talk to Helen? It was a torment she suffered just at a time when she was starting a new job, one that intimidated her in several ways.

I don't need a torment like this—I don't deserve it.

By the top of the stairs, Helen had worked herself up into a frenzy of indignation. She pushed open the door leading to the highest tier and declared, "Now we shall get to the bottom of this!"

And it was just as she had feared. No one stood on the stretch of balcony where she'd seen the girl a moment ago. She slipped away yet again.

"Mrs. O'Neill! Mrs. O'Neill, what are you doing?"

Belle da Costa Greene stood in the middle of the room, and even from this distance Helen could tell that she was shocked.

"Miss Greene, there is someone up here, someone who doesn't belong," said Helen, her voice echoing.

Her employer moved toward the stairs, immediately concerned. "Who? When did you see him?"

"Not a man, a young girl."

With that, Belle froze. "A girl in here? I've observed no girl admitted to the library today. I can't think why a young female would be here."

Oh, no, this isn't going to go at all well for me.

Helen cleared her throat. There was no choice now, no going back. "I did see her, Miss, and I've seen her before, outside the library. She was standing up here, looking down, and in the time it took me to reach her, she must have made it to the other stairs."

"Well, let's have a look then."

There was no mistaking the grimness underlying Belle's tone. Flushed with frustration, Helen made the rounds of the square balcony facing the books as Belle made a thorough search of both winding staircases. There was no sign of the girl. Worse, their activities had drawn the attention of Mr. Lawrence, the guard, watching in confusion as the two women hurried this way and that.

"Do either of the staircases connect below to other passageways, to that tunnel leading to the house?" asked Helen, desperate, when both had returned to the main floor.

"No, of course not. It's not that sort of tunnel. You don't work in a maze, Mrs. O'Neill. There was no one up there, you must have just seen a shadow."

Helen said, "She wasn't a shadow."

Belle called out, "Mr. Lawrence, could you join us over here?" When the guard had made it to their side, she said, "Has a girl come to the library today? Could you describe her, Mrs. O'Neill?"

"She is about twenty years of age, very slim, dark brown hair parted down the middle, wearing a full-skirted light-colored dress with blue ribbons."

Mr. Lawrence guffawed, then caught himself and said, "No, Ma'am, no one fitting that description was admitted to the library today."

"Thank you, Mr. Lawrence, you may return to your duties in the rotunda." Her tone was icy, but it wasn't the guard she was angry with. She waited until Mr. Lawrence had left before launching in.

"Mrs. O'Neill, I don't know what is going on here, certainly not intrusions from young maidens in white dresses. You were recommended to me as sensible—imminently sensible—and hard working and resourceful, as well as being exceptionally talented in your handling of artifacts and valuables. But this week, only your second week with us, you've been distracted, disorganized, you've acted oddly, and now, with Mr. Morgan on the premises, you raise the alarm with this foolishness. Thank God he isn't aware of this."

Her cheeks flame, her stomach churning, Helen said, "I am

very sorry, Miss. All I can say is, this won't happen again. I am appreciative of the opportunity."

Belle took a deep breath, the worse of her temper passed. Guardedly, she said, "Perhaps we should both return to our duties and discuss this further at the end of the day."

"Yes, Miss."

Helen made her way back to her worktable, fighting waves of nausea. She was horrified over what just occurred. But the reprimand from Belle wasn't the worst of it. There were things to be faced here and implications that couldn't be more disturbing.

Am I losing my mind?

Her mother called it "away with the fairies." That was the expression: On the more benign end of the spectrum, it meant being muddle-headed and thinking of matters far away and, on the darker end, being stark raving mad.

But Helen had never felt herself slipping into madness before, not even when she was in the worst of her grief over Sean. Would it strike now, in her mid-thirties, out of nowhere, and in the shape of a young girl who came and went?

She looked down at her fingers, trembling on the edge of her worktable. There was another explanation, one that she recoiled from with all her being. Helen could be in her right mind, but the girl who kept appearing before her was not a living, breathing person. She was a spirit—a ghost—that only Helen could see.

Words said decades ago reverberated in her head, those from the mouth of a furious father: "I won't have you bringing fairy tales of the bog into our home. It's bad enough you take it to heart, but to put it about that Little Helen could see spirit beings out among the people—or that only she can do special tasks."

It's not true. There aren't any such things as aes sidhe. I'm not one of them!

The undeniable question rose: But what about her gift with her hands, the gift that surfaced time and again?

In desperation, Helen clung to something said much more recently. Her superior at the Metropolitan Museum of Art told her one day, "Mrs. O'Neill, I was speaking of your special talent with a friend of mine who's a medical man. He said he knows of other cases of exceptional coordination between hand and eye. We're indeed fortunate to have you."

That was it—that must be it. "Exceptional coordination between hand and eye, exceptional coordination between hand and eye." She repeated it until her panic subsided. Helen wouldn't think any more about the girl, or madness, or *aes sidhe.* She *must* return to her work. It was so painful to anger Miss Greene, she had to repair the damage. Nothing else mattered.

Helen forced herself to examine the back cover of the Lindau Gospels. It had been removed for study, to be reattached after any needed attention given. Through will power, Helen drove everything else from her mind and devoted herself to her work. She heard doors open and shut off the rotunda, and male voices. Helen prayed that Mr. Morgan wouldn't come in the main library this afternoon. She was in no fit state to present herself. Thankfully, he did not, and the abrupt dying down of noise indicated J. P. Morgan had left.

It was Belle da Costa Greene who returned, her expression somber. "I know I said we should speak more at the end of day, but I find myself needing to receive some last-minute appointments here. It's always like that when Mr. Morgan comes back to the library. Fresh business presents itself." Her eyes strayed to Helen's notebook. "I see you've made more progress this afternoon. Why don't you go home—it's after five o'clock—and get some rest this weekend? We shall see what Monday brings."

"Yes, thank you, Miss. I do want to continue with my work."

"I might have spoken too harshly before. We're under some strain here, you see. It was a difficult time for Mr. Morgan in

Washington, D.C." She hesitated, then said, quietly, "He's much misunderstood."

I know how he feels, thought Helen grimly.

She finished her notes for the day and prepared to leave. She peered up at the balconies of bookshelves before she departed the room. No sign of her.

Outside, it was a still, cold night, with no fresh snow on the ground. Helen walked briskly up Thirty-Sixth Street, trying not to look too closely at anyone else on the sidewalks. Which did not turn out to necessary, there was no sign of her girlish nemesis. She saw only people milling about who were well bundled for the weather.

Reaching the corner, Helen took a last look at the house itself, which surely must be at its height of activity with Mr. Morgan home. Every window showed light inside; the building throbbed with life. Outside the wall facing Madison Avenue, against the frozen thinning ivy, she spotted something a little unusual: a pair of people walking slowly, from the back of the house toward its front along the ground. It was an odd path to use, with the sidewalk so close. The snow could ruin shoes.

Helen took a step closer to the Morgan house to try to see the two of them more clearly. They were uneven in size. One was tall and wide, the other small and thin. One was a man, and one was a woman....

She took another step north on Madison Avenue, and a few more, nearly stumbling on the icy sidewalk. This was as close to them as she could get.

Helen clapped a gloved hand over her mouth. By the light streaming from the mansion's windows, she could make out who the two people were. J. P. Morgan walked alongside the girl, in the shadow of his house. His head was tilted down, as if to hear better what she said. He was nodding in agreement. And beside him, her hand resting on his arm, she tripped along lightly, her mouth moving as if deep in conversation.

CHAPTER 7

Helen barely spoke to her family that night, making the excuse of yet another headache. Nor could she eat more than a few bites of food, her appetite vanished. At the first opportunity, she fled to her bedroom, where she crawled into bed and pulled the covers high without getting into her nightclothes first.

The girl was real—she had to be. It was unmistakably her walking on the grounds of the house with its owner, J. P. Morgan. But why then couldn't they find her in the main library? Belle and Helen had searched it thoroughly, and Mr. Lawrence swore that a girl of her description never entered the building. How could she have gotten past him—or made her way up to the highest balcony?

The alternative: She was *not* real but a spirit, and her unearthly form was one that two people could see: Helen O'Neill and J. P. Morgan.

Tears squeezed from her eyes as Helen huddled under the covers. Who could she talk to—a priest in Confession? Ghosts were evil, perhaps even demonic, she'd been taught. She shrank from opening herself up to that. A family member? There was no one. Only two people had ever perceived the possibilities that existed within Helen. Her differences—what set her apart. Her mother … and her husband.

"Sean, can you help me?" she whispered. "I wish you could help me."

Helen could imagine what he'd say, "Ah, darling, I'd love to help you. But what can we do about our wee problem? I'm dead and buried."

With all that she had been through, she couldn't hold back her memories, those she had learned to put in a corner and examine rarely.

Helen Connolly met Sean O'Neill when she was eighteen years old. It was at a St. Valentine's party thrown at a dilapidated city dance hall in the Bronx, not in Morrisania but Woodlawn, another Irish stronghold. She'd never been to the place before. Frances, a young woman Helen worked with at the seamstress's, Mrs. O'Malley's, begged her to come, because Frances's parents wouldn't let *her* attend without a friend as chaperone, seeing there would be many boys eager for dances.

Helen wasn't much for dancing, but she agreed. In fact she welcomed the invitation, as she did any opportunity to feel like other young women. It might have been her natural shyness, of being a small, self-contained member of a loud family. Or it might have been something else. While never being ostracized, she was far from popular. Something held people back. Helen heard other girls her age talking about things she didn't know about, didn't seem to be experiencing. She attracted no beaus and while other eighteen-year-olds were planning their weddings, Helen had only her job at Mrs. O'Malley's. It was a fine job, but still. She wanted to venture into the middle of the stream, where the other girls swam. But she never could.

When Helen was thirteen and a strange cramping feeling made her double up in the washroom, she was not frightened but thrilled. The bright red blood spattering her undergarments meant she was just like every girl. Helen never complained about her time of the month. She silently celebrated it and longed for more milestones like it.

I'm a normal human, I'm like everyone else.

For this dance, she hoped for another sort of new experience, while having only a vague idea of what it could be. She picked out her best dress, a pink one. Its color brightened her pale complexion and set off her long blonde hair. But it was more than that—the fit was excellent. She was nervous about that, but it was a pleasing nervousness.

Helen worried that her family would have a lot of questions for her, criticize her for going to a Woodlawn dance dressed like this, but they were busy with their own affairs and only too happy that Helen had formed a Saturday night plan with a friend.

A small, amateurish band played music inside the dance hall, which was packed with young people. Frances was whisked away for dances almost immediately, while Helen received no offers for the first half-hour. She stood on the edge of a group of similarly overlooked young women, trying to prevent herself from sinking into self-pity.

A stirring in the crowd made the young women next to Helen perk up. "Oh, look, it's the Belfast Boys," said one, her voice carrying.

Helen had heard about these young men from her brothers. It was a nickname given to a group that arrived in America in the last five to ten years from Belfast in County Ulster. Increasing strife between Catholic and Protestant had set loose another round of immigrants. The Belfast Boys lived in Brooklyn or the west side of Manhattan, not Queens or the Bronx. And, of greatest interest to the young women pressed against the wall of the dance hall, they were known to be pretty wild.

With a swagger as if he owned the place, a tall redhead walked through the crowd before tapping a pretty young woman on the shoulder he thought worthy of his attentions. Magically, she was free to join him on the dance floor. There were four other men in his wake, fanning out to boldly survey what Woodlawn had to offer.

How presumptuous—who do they think they are?

Helen refused to look at the arrogant newcomers, eagerness wouldn't pour from her like it did from the other females. Instead she fixed her eyes on a framed photograph propped next to a table of Assemblyman Al Smith, the pride of Irish New Yorkers. Which is why she didn't see Sean O'Neill until he was planted in front of her.

She glanced down at a pair of large scruffy shoes. Looking up, she took in a tall man of about twenty-one with brown hair and blue-gray eyes fringed with dark eyelashes A long scar over his left eye marred what would have been quite a handsome face. This was a Belfast Boy who'd been banged about.

"Would you care for a dance, Miss?" he said with a sweeping bow, his manner that of a man sure of acceptance.

In the five seconds it took her to say yes, Sean's gaze, which darted to the side of and behind Helen's neat blonde head, perhaps searching for his next partner, zeroed in on her and stayed there.

"I suppose one dance would be acceptable," she said coolly.

His eyebrows shot up, and the man, introducing himself as Sean O'Neill, led her out on the floor. They weren't perfectly matched, as Sean was eight inches taller than her and had to bend down quite a bit to partner her. She wasn't a polished dancer. Twice Helen bumped into him.

At the end of the dance, she fully expected him to shoot off to find someone else, but instead he suggested they drink some punch.

After sipping the dreadful punch, Helen said politely, "What brings you to the Bronx?"

"Ah, we were planning to spend Saturday night in Brooklyn,

as usual, but we heard that the prettiest girls were to be found here."

Disappointed by his glibness, Helen said, "I'm sure there are plenty of beauties in Brooklyn that would fit your bill."

He laughed, a high, rich lilting laugh, not what she expected of him, and said, "Oh, there are, there are." He ran his eyes up and down her figure appreciatively. "None such a dainty little miss as you."

His boldness shocked her, but she felt a wriggle of pleasure too. At that moment, Helen had not too high a regard for Mr. Sean O'Neill, but a new desire stirred. She tried out an alluring smile—it was her first ever, and a tremendous success. Sean stayed firmly by her side all night, dance after dance, his hands creeping around her waist or lingering on her shoulders whenever a dance move allowed.

It couldn't have been more obvious that Sean had tried out all these advances before with other girls, and she suspected they worked. Helen had it in her mind to do what other young women did, to feel things that they felt with a man. Sean O'Neill would be an expert guide. And she was warming to his easy patter, all in a Northern Ireland accent she found highly attractive.

"Maybe we should take the air?" he suggested, a hopeful gleam in his eyes, though he tilted his head back at the same time, as if girding himself for a rebuff.

"Maybe we should, Mr. O'Neill."

Outside, Sean put his arm through hers and led her down the block, toward a row of quiet houses fronted by thick trees.

I'm about to find out what it means when a man takes liberties.

Helen, with her background—protective family and religious training—should never have agreed to be alone with a man twice her size who was virtually a stranger. She had no experience with men, hadn't had one ask to hold her hand or venture a chaste kiss on her cheek. To make up for lost time, she was ready to leap forward a dozen steps in the game of men and women with this Belfast Boy.

He stopped and whirled around suddenly, as if he couldn't wait any longer, and reached for her hand, pulling her in closer. She went forward gladly, tilting up her face to be kissed. But he didn't do that.

"Your hand," he breathed in surprise. "It's so tiny and ... so precious."

That wasn't the word she was expecting. She expected Sean to engulf her in kisses and rough caresses, but instead he looked down at her, all serious.

"Miss Connolly, there's moonlight in your hair, and you look so beautiful. You're like someone I know."

She shook her head. "We've never met before."

"Perhaps it's someone I heard about."

"I hardly think my fame has made it to Brooklyn."

"No, I have it," he said slowly. "It's the stories of the enchanted people. The stories of the *aes sidhe*."

Helen broke away, horrified, but he caught her with both hands, and he was far stronger. "You can't get away from me, Miss Connolly—I would do anything to have a girl like you. Anything at all."

"I'm not *enchanted*."

He laughed. "The rest of the world is drab and boring and mean and here you are, a magical, beautiful creature, and you don't want to be? I don't believe it."

He bent down, and Helen could see that he was a little afraid of her right before he kissed her. It was the tenderest kiss in the world, and in that instant, she was lost.

Their relationship was set that night. The wonder of finding someone new and exciting wore off, as it must. They'd argue, they'd criticize each other. But at his core, Sean was captivated by Helen as no one else had ever been, and he coaxed from her all that was special. The most important thing to her was that he accepted her, just as she was.

LYING in her bed years later, Helen wiped the tears away. Enough of this. She was the one who must struggle to understand. There was something extraordinary about the girl in the cream-colored dress. But the newest development revealed she was not the only one who could see her

There was also J. P. Morgan.

After breakfast on Saturday, Helen knocked on her brother Stephen's door. She was not eager to lay herself open to his probing questions, his sarcasm, but she hadn't a choice. In their family, Stephen was the one who read the newspapers and attended all sorts of lectures as well as concerts.

"I would like to know all that you know about J. P. Morgan," she said as humbly as she could manage.

"Aren't you the one who's in a position to have knowledge of the man?"

Helen thought he was about to rebuff her. Instead he suggested tea downstairs.

The kitchen was Siobhan's domain, but it was between the cleaning up after one meal and the preparing of the next, so the little table with its checkered tablecloth was available. After Helen had put a hot tea in his hands, her brother told her what he knew.

"The Congressional hearings he appeared before, they gave him a rough time, from what I understand. They're convinced that the way our country is run needs to be changed. No more rich men like J. P. Morgan pulling all the strings. One senator accused him of engineering the panic of 1907 so that he could pick up the failing companies for a cheap price."

That wasn't the way Belle explained it. "Do you think he did such a thing?"

"No, but I agree that the time has passed for men like Morgan to be more powerful than any president of the United States. He and his friends make deals in closed rooms with no one knowing what happens. It's not democracy."

Helen thought of Morgan's sumptuous study. Perhaps his critics had a point. But this wasn't the kind of insight that would most help her.

Cautiously, she said, "What of his character besides matters of finance?"

Stephen laughed. "He's the man who bought out Andrew Carnegie to create U.S. Steel, who put together the financing for our nation's railroads and lends money all over the world, How could anything besides finance matter?"

"What if I were to tell you that he's a leading Episcopalian, that he's a devout man?"

"Yes, I think I read that." Stephen stifled a yawn.

Helen decided to take the plunge.

"Or what about the fact that Mr. Morgan believes in astrology—he is a member of something called the Zodiac Club—and had an artist paint them across his ceiling. *And* he has audiences with psychics?"

"An Episcopalian who believes in psychics? God preserve us from the Protestants!"

Helen sipped her tea. This wasn't getting her anywhere. But then, as if a spout turned on, Stephen relayed what he knew.

"I know Morgan has a yacht, the biggest one in America, and the gossip writers say he is a ladies' man. Incredible, with that nose. Just shows what a fortune will do, besides being able to collect all the paintings and statues and rare books he can lay hands on and stick in that library you work for. Of course he has a family, one son and some daughters. The daughters travel with him when he sails across the Atlantic back and forth, back and forth. I don't think he had any children by his first wife."

Helen's fingers tightened around her cup.

"First wife?"

"Yes, I think so. I think there was one. When he was young. She died before long."

Helen had never believed for a minute that people came back from the dead, but there was something about the way J. P. Morgan walked beside the girl, his attentiveness.

He looked down at her as a husband would.

"How do we find out about his first wife?" she pressed.

Stephen studied his sister. "We don't, not here in the Bronx on a Saturday."

"The public library?"

"Closed on the weekends."

"There must be some way, Stephen. Think. I need to know."

Her plea poured out of her in a rush, and now she was exposed to him. Her oldest brother, John Jr., was one for bear hugs and slaps on the arms and friendly hair pulls; Stephen was never one for laying hands on people. But he reached across the table now and grabbed his sister's arm, the spoon from his tea clattering across the tablecloth. "What is it, Helen? What's wrong? You're acting as if your life depends on learning about a woman who's been dead at least fifty years."

Helen gasped as another piece of this puzzle slotted in. *That* would explain the girl's clothes—why she was wearing a dress and styling her hair from a different time. It was fifty years ago.

"Stop it," said Stephen, "you're frightening me. We all know that the job is doing something terrible to you. You're silent, when you do speak it's about headaches, you've lost your color. This obsession with the man's family, it doesn't make any sense." Stephen swallowed. "Has he been unkind to you, or done anything untoward?"

"Mr. Morgan hasn't said a word to me."

"Helen, tell me what's upsetting you. I swear I won't breathe a word to anyone."

"Swear to Mother, Mary, and Joseph?" she pressed, feeling

as if they were children again.

"I do."

She didn't feel the same excitement as she had when sharing this with her sister. Perhaps because that confiding had gone so wrong. But Helen took the plunge and told her brother about the sightings of the girl, every one of them, including seeing her walking with J. P. Morgan. He listened, at times shaking his head or grimacing, but he didn't say a word.

When she'd finished, Stephen said, "Helen, I think it's obvious. This girl is Morgan's mistress. That's why she lingers outside his house, how she found her way into the library, and why she's walking with him, arm in arm."

"No, no, that isn't it."

"What else?" He stared at her, then hunched over and put his face in his hands. "You think this girl is Morgan's dead wife, come back to the living in order to haunt him. Oh, Lord, Helen. Oh, Lord. You're away with the fairies now."

She pushed away from the table, her face scarlet. "I *knew* you wouldn't understand."

Helen stalked out of the kitchen. Stephen ran after her, pulling on her arm as he said, "You have to get hold of yourself."

"Leave me alone," she hissed, yanking her arm away.

"You think you're the only one in the family who suffers? Do you? Poor Helen, who became a widow and never smiles, won't set foot in Brooklyn because of her memories. What about me? Stephen couldn't get a position at Fordham University and lives with his brother and sister, hard on forty."

His words hurt terribly, but she could see, for the first time, that her brother had suffered in life too. A nerve jumped on the side of his cheek as he said, "I have to hear about Fordham day in and day out, look upon it too. There've been other disappointments—and people—you know nothing about, no one does. It's always been about Helen under this roof."

This astonished her, that he could say such a thing, even in anger. She was the odd youngest daughter, small and plain, always overlooked.

"I've never been a burden to anyone here," she insisted.

"Ma worried about you night and day after Sean died. She was sick with the cancer for years, but I think she held on, defying all the doctors, until she knew that you were on your feet again, working in Manhattan, that you would be all right. Only then could she let go."

"Don't say that." Helen covered her eyes, as if she couldn't bear to look at him when he spoke of such matters.

John Jr.'s teenagers came crashing into the kitchen, grabbing some provisions for a day of ice skating. They paid no notice to their aunt and uncle, their wounded faces.

"Why won't Pa ask Mr. Ferguson if we could get a ride in his motorcar?"

"You know what he'll say. 'I won't ask favors of a Scot!'"

The boys charged out again, and a calmer Stephen said, "I'm sorry, Helen. But you're being selfish and you're wrapping yourself up in dangerous foolishness."

Helen backed out of the kitchen, shaking her head.

The fight with Stephen filled her with as much regret as that with Sister Bernadette. What she was going through at Morgan's library, it was destroying her peace of mind, her health, and her place in her family. But hating it wasn't making it stop.

I have to learn the truth, that's the only way to end it.

Stephen's solution, a mistress, wasn't correct, for a dozen reasons, foremost that the girl seemed to very much want to communicate with Helen. What was her part in all this?

The next time she appeared, Helen wouldn't hesitate, wouldn't permit her to slip away. She was going to get the truth from her—if necessary, by force.

CHAPTER 8

Monday dawned, Helen's third one at Morgan's library, and with it, grim determination. Helen dressed and left early for Manhattan, to avoid sharing the kitchen with Stephen.

Walking to the subway, Helen relaxed a trifle, feeling the bright sun on her face. It was one of those bizarre days that New York City throws up every winter season: an oasis of beckoning sun and caressing warmth. The robins sang full throated on the tree branches, as if celebrating spring. This reprieve wouldn't last long, but the red-breasted birds could be forgiven their confusion.

Just outside Pennsylvania Station, a smiling crowd huddled around a man who wore his Santa Claus suit with pride, ringing a bell and calling out to those hurrying to their jobs in the city to spare a coin for the poor. The Salvation Army truck rumbled behind him.

In a friendly competition, another "Santa" strode by, holding a sign saying, "Come See the Christmas Tree in Madison Park." Heads turned, intrigued by something new. "First time the City of New York has raised a tree for the public," he boomed. "You don't want to miss it, folks. It's sixty feet tall. Come to Madison Park!"

This burst of Yuletide celebration was a continuation of the spirit of the Connolly house all weekend. Even in her fraught state, Helen was aware of the excitement bubbling within her niece, Rose. For the tenth time, she made Helen promise to be by her side on Christmas Eve night, when they lit the red candle and placed it in the front window of the house, facing the street.

This was the favorite Christmas custom of Helen's mother, Anne, and children and grandchildren honored her by making it the centerpiece of Christmas Eve each year. The red candle was lit to show the way for Mary and Joseph, struggling to find a stable in Bethlehem. But its other meaning was to serve as a sign of welcome for anyone who might pass by, be it friend, relative, or stranger in need of hospitality. The youngest in each family lit the red candle, so went the tradition. Last year, Rose and her aunt huddled inside, watching the wax slowly melt while they drank hot cocoa, far beyond the time the others drifted away.

Today I am the one in need.

Her spirits sank the closer she got to J. P. Morgan's house and library. She struggled to hold on to her courage in the coming confrontation.

She kept wondering, Why had she been marked out for such a frightening ordeal—why couldn't this position at the library, one that so many might well envy, have proceeded with any normality? One possible reason whispered in Helen's ear as she walked up Madison Avenue and Morgan's brick house eased into view. There wasn't much that was "normal" about J. P. Morgan. He was larger than life, as was his collection, housed in what looked like a Roman emperor's palace on the outside and a Renaissance prince's on the inside. And these treasures he drew to him from every corner of the globe, they brought their own mysteries with them, perhaps.

She glanced warily at the side of the house facing Madison,

but there was only a tough-faced gardener to be seen, sorting some of the yellowing ivy tangled toward the back. She continued through the library's brass doors, to be met again with pungent cigar smoke. Mr. Morgan was here. Yes, he certainly did consider this his headquarters, more than his bank on Wall Street.

Helen's nerves tightened to the breaking point when she entered Belle da Costa Greene's office, a place she would have liked to avoid but for the necessity of hanging up her coat in the corner cloakroom. To her relief, Belle was absent.

After scanning the balconies above to make sure she was not being observed in the main library, Helen settled in at her worktable and pushed on with her study of the Lindau Gospels. After a time, she heard Belle's heels clicking across the rotunda, but she woman herself did not appear. The guards admitted two men whose loud salutations echoed, and she recognized Mr. Morgan's gruff voice in welcoming them, although she could not see him from where she sat.

Helen again pictured the couple walking along the house Friday evening. What man would parade his mistress along the side of his own house—in view of his wife on the other side of the windows? That wasn't the truth of it; he wasn't her seducer. Morgan had been listening with close and respectful attention to the girl as she walked beside him, as a husband would. Perhaps this was the only place they could talk, away from his family? The point was, the girl had successful conversed with him while never reaching that point with Helen. Helen shifted uneasily in her chair as a new thought occurred: Were they talking about Helen Friday night?

It was a ridiculous notion—she was but a low-level worker here. Why would a Bronx widow be a topic of interest to J. P. Morgan and his mysterious companion?

Yet as the minutes crawled by, the idea took deeper root in Helen's mind. Failing to speak to her, the girl had gone to

Morgan. She couldn't shake off the suspicion, no matter how hard she tried. Helen set down her pencil after failing to finish a sentence about the Lindau Gospels. These morbid preoccupations were unbearable.

Voices rose again, with the word "Keens" said by one of the men. Helen knew they were trooping out again to J. P. Morgan's mutton and steak destination. After a few minutes, it grew very quiet in the rotunda.

Mr. Morgan's study might be empty now—and unlocked.

It was a thought scratching away at her, like the mouse in the walls of their house last year. If she could manage a way into the study, she could search for clues to the girl inside. No matter Stephen's scorn, Helen persisted in thinking it a strong possibility that the girl was the first Mrs. Morgan. Belle da Costa Greene's office contained photographs, might not Morgan's?

This was madness, to invade her employer's privacy in such a way. Yet if she were to attempt it, now was the time. Yesterday the guards had secured their own lunch while Morgan dined. Belle seemed preoccupied with her work. It was now or never.

A tremendous excitement sang in Helen's ears as she made her way to the opening to the rotunda. She knew this was an action completely uncharacteristic of her. It could even be a crime, and she'd never committed a crime in her whole life. But Helen couldn't go back and sit at the table.

Just as she'd hoped, none of the guards patrolled the rotunda. The way was clear. And Mr. Morgan's office door hung ajar a few inches.

She darted across the marble floor. Before pushing open the door, Helen peeked inside and made sure it was empty. Then she edged into the plush space, pulling the door closed to just a few inches as she had seen before.

It didn't take long for her to realize there were no family

photos of J. P. Morgan or any female in the study, just the portrait of the millionaire hanging over the fireplace

But leaving after just a minute seemed like a waste of this opportunity. Helen approached the huge desk of J. P. Morgan, knowing that to examine it was an unforgivable violation. Nothing on its top to be seen but some bound books and papers in a leather folder, along with a thick crystal ashtray.

Her fingers slippery with perspiration, Helen pulled open the heavy top drawer. Files and papers. She didn't know what to look for. She closed it and pulled open the next one. Still nothing that offered answers. Yet somehow her damp fingers touched the rim of a frame tucked into the middle drawer.

Helen pulled it out carefully.

The photograph within the frame was of faded sepia, taken long, long ago. Helen felt her knees begin to quiver as she stared at the faces in the photograph: Beside an impossibly young Morgan was a young woman with brown hair parted in the middle, her expression resolute, dignified, and compassionate. This was the girl who appeared to Helen. A fragile column, clipped from a larger newspaper page, was slipped into the frame. She unfolded it with care.

"Amelia Morgan, beloved wife of John Pierpont Morgan, passed away on February 17, 1862..."

Helen lowered the frame and the obituary, her head spinning. She had suspected this, but to see the girl's face...?

"Mrs. O'Neill!"

The voice of Belle da Costa Greene smashed through the silence. She charged across the study, Mr. Lawrence the guard peering behind her. Belle's eyes were crackling with anger—more than that. With outrage.

"How dare you come in here without permission—and how dare you touch Mr. Morgan's personal photographs?" she shouted. "Are you here to steal from him?"

"No, Miss Greene, no!" Helen pleaded. "I would never do that."

Belle said, "Stand still while I search you. Mr. Lawrence, go through her worktable and bring me her satchel, to see if she has already secreted anything. I will have to do a full inventory as well." Belle wrung her hands. "If you've done anything to the Landau Gospels...."

"I haven't taken anything, I promise you."

Belle snorted her disbelief. Helen went through with being searched, a humiliation she found agonizing, all the more because she knew that Belle da Costa Greene had every reason to feel betrayed. She made no protest when Belle marched her to the small cloakroom, muttering, "I should be sending for the police, but first I'll talk to Mr. Morgan."

Being fired if not arrested were distinct possibilities, Helen knew. Yet she kept coming back to the truth of the photograph. The first wife of J. P. Morgan haunted Madison Avenue and the library. But she had no way to prove it. Who would believe Helen when she said she had seen the girl in the photo walking and talking in 1912?

The lock clicked, and the cloakroom door swung open.

"Mrs. O'Neill, please come out now," said Belle tersely.

Blinking in the light after so long in the dark cloakroom, Helen emerged. She wanted so much to be understood—and forgiven—by Belle, without any idea of how to achieve that.

"Mr. Morgan would like to speak to you."

Helen took a step back, ready to return to the cloakroom. "I can't," she whispered. Although she knew Morgan was the one who might have answers, it was too terrifying a prospect.

"Oh, but you will. It's either that—or straight to the nearest police."

Belle led her to the doorway of J. P. Morgan's study, now occupied by the man himself, sitting behind the massive desk she had searched before. There was no one else in the room.

"I'll see her alone, Miss Greene," he said in that low, gruff voice.

Looking surprised, Belle backed away, closing the door behind her.

"Sit down, Mrs. O'Neill."

It took all her courage to walk the distance from the door to that of the chair opposite J. P. Morgan. By the time she had made it halfway, Helen realized that the intensity of his black eyes held not anger but curiosity.

"I'm very sorry for what I did, Mr. Morgan," she said, her voice a croak.

He waved his hand, as if in dismissal. Helen sat down. He said nothing, and she was too daunted to speak again. The fire hissed and crackled in the room. Even more than when he stood in the doorway to the library, she felt his weariness.

"You won't be losing your position, Mrs. O'Neill," he said. "I'll inform Miss Greene. Nor will I be pressing charges with the police."

Her shoulders sagged with relief. But after a moment, she cleared her throat and said, "Why?"

"You saw us—me and Memie," he asked. "Walking by the house on Friday."

Memie. That must be his name for Amelia.

It should have sent her into panic or prayers, this admission from Mr. Morgan that he walked the earth with a dead wife. But Helen sat up straighter in her chair. "Yes, Sir. Yes, I did."

He said quietly, "I didn't think anyone else could see her. I thought I was the only one. When people see me walking with her, nodding or talking, they assume I'm just being eccentric."

"I was afraid I was the only one who saw her." It burst out of Helen's mouth and he nodded, as if that answered a question for him.

"She scared you," he said. "Memie scared you."

Helen nodded.

"She never wanted to. That's the difference, you see? It was quite a shock, don't get me wrong, but I was so glad that she returned to me, after all these years, that first time. I couldn't be frightened of her."

To Helen's astonishment, J. P. Morgan's eyes glistened with tears.

He said, haltingly, "She was sick when we married. Tuberculosis. I had to carry her down the stairs for the ceremony. I thought I could cure her. The best doctors, a warm climate. I was twenty-four years old, you see."

He closed his eyes and his shoulders shuddered. He muttered, "She died four months after our wedding."

Filled with compassion, Helen said, "I was only married to Mr. O'Neill eighteen months. I understand, Sir."

J. P. Morgan opened his eyes. "Yes, I know."

Helen stiffened. "I see. Miss Greene talked about my husband with you?"

"No." His dark eyes flickered. "Memie did."

Helen's hands clutched at her throat. This terrified her; it was a violation of her marriage, of her own soul, that a spirit of the dead should have knowledge of Sean.

"What are you saying?" she demanded. "*What do you mean?*"

"She wants to help you."

"How?" she said loudly. Helen no longer spoke to him with the respect a man like J. P. Morgan was accustomed to. He was not at all bothered by it. "What can she do for me? I don't understand!"

But Morgan, having come this far, now hesitated. He seemed unsure of his words, or whether they should even be spoken.

Watching his struggle, the answer hit Helen with the force of a blow, sucking the breath from her.

Just as Memie came back to Morgan, someone else could come back to me.

"Oh—oh," she cried. "It's Sean. She's going to bring me *Sean.* I'll see him again, as you saw your wife again."

He raised a hand, his knuckles swollen and his fingertips yellowed. "I'm not sure," he said. "It could be what will occur. Or not."

Tears sprang into Helen's eyes. "Oh, thank you, Sir. I'm so grateful," she babbled. "I can't tell you how grateful I am."

"I don't know for certain, Mrs. O'Neill. Please, please, you mustn't count on this."

But Helen didn't take in his words, the joy of this chance offered her was too overwhelming. She turned in her chair, looking this way and that. "Will it be here, in your study or the library, or out on Madison Avenue?"

"My instinct says no. When Memie first came to me, it was on Fourteenth Street, where we courted. That was her parents' house."

Helen clapped her hands. "Of course, that makes perfect sense. Yes!"

As Helen abandoned her composure, J. P. Morgan seemed to regain his. He scrutinized her, tapping his fingers on his desk. "I'm sure you are the only other person who can see Memie, I just don't know why that would be."

"I've no idea, Sir. Why do you think she appeared to you?"

"To help me. As to how she manages to appear to me, that I don't know. I have not set out to make it happen, I didn't pay for seances or necromancers." He shifted in his chair. "But I have followed through on my curiosity on such matters over the years. My endeavor is to get to an understanding of what is unknowable." He swiveled in his chair, looking into the fire. "Two years ago, I saw a man in Turkey on the way to one of my excavation trips, he brought with him a recommendation from the Black Princesses, Militsa and Anastasia of Montenegro. They were the same women who introduced Grigori Rasputin to the Czar and Czarina. It was an unforgettable night, he dangled possibilities I'd thought impossible." He sighed. "But I don't know."

Helen felt herself grow cold as the whiff of the occult floated across J. P. Morgan's study.

His voice even stronger, Morgan said, "I wasn't going to say anything as yet, because I'm just not sure of anything, Mrs. O'Neill. But when Miss Greene caught you with Memie's photograph, I knew what drove you to do that. I felt I had to tell you what I know. Wouldn't be fair to stay silent."

"You can't know how grateful I am."

He shifted some of the papers around on his desk. "I may not see you again for a while, Mrs. O'Neill. I'm booked on a cruise at the end of the year. Egypt. Then Europe."

Feeling the audience was at an end, Helen stood. "I wish you good health and every blessing, Mr. Morgan."

Looking at her somberly, J. P. Morgan said, "It can be difficult, confronted with your past. It's not been easy for me. You might want to think carefully about this."

"But the chance of it— the chance!"

J. P. Morgan sighed. "I understand. You will be uppermost in my prayers, Mrs. O'Neill."

CHAPTER 9

"You look like you have a fever. Your cheeks are red, and there's a brightness in your eyes."

That was the greeting Helen received when she arrived home in Morrisania a couple of hours earlier than usual. Her sister-in-law even held out a palm to feel her forehead, but Helen playfully swatted it away.

I haven't felt this light in years, as if I'm floating.

"I'm absolutely fine," she reassured Siobhan. "I was just sent home early because it's Christmas Eve tomorrow. I won't be needed for the rest of the week, but I'm paid all the same."

Helen didn't share the true reason for leaving Morgan's library in the mid-afternoon. It was true that she had the week off at full pay. Belle da Costa Greene had informed her as much, looking greatly puzzled. However, Belle was always loyal to J. P. Morgan, and she followed his wishes. Helen had no idea what he told Belle about her, perhaps she never would.

After her conversation with J. P. Morgan, her feelings for the library changed completely. She had new appreciation for the beauty of its architecture, the talent of Harry Siddons Mowbray, the artist who painted the ceiling murals. She eagerly scanned the upper balconies as she prepared to leave the main library.

Now she sought out visitations, though admittedly the thought of Sean O'Neill striding in front of the upper bookshelves seemed remote. Also Morgan said he would find her in a place he associated with Helen.

To her surprise, when she glanced up at the rotunda mural painting, the grouping that included Orpheus, the demi-god no longer reminded her of Sean. He was just an ordinary dark-haired man with a harp, not her roughly handsome Belfast Boy.

Outside, on Thirty-Sixth Street and Madison Avenue, still bathed in unseasonal warmth, no apparitions appeared either. But Helen knew that Sean had never been near here with her; she needed to figure out a place they frequented.

Which wouldn't be the Connollys' present house, she thought on the way home. They had moved into it seven years ago, shortly after Rose was born. When Sean came courting, the Connollys lived in a smaller house in Morrisania. Helen intended to go there first thing in the morning.

First there was the night to get through. This dinner was unlike any that Helen had enjoyed since she began work at Morgan's library—and even earlier than that, truth to tell. She dove into the food on her plate, laying on the compliments for Siobhan's breaded chicken with potatoes and cabbage. She asked her nephews about school and teased Rose about setting the candle in the window.

"What shall we say to a person who comes inside after seeing our red candle?" Helen asked. "They might want to eat all the food in the house."

"Oh, no—no!" sad Rose, giggling.

"You're in fine fettle tonight, Helen," said John Jr., with an approving nod. The light gleamed off the top of his scalp; his blonde hair wasn't just thinning. Her brother was going bald. There was a layer of flesh under his chin she'd not noticed before as well.

We're all getting old. It was a sobering thought amid her newfound happiness, and she quickly pushed it away.

The other discordant note was struck by Stephen, who didn't comment about the change in Helen but watched her throughout dinner, with a scrutiny she didn't welcome. It was tempting to tell Stephen everything, but on top of the bizarre nature of her conversation with J. P. Morgan, and the proof she'd received that the dead could come back to comfort the living, was the thought that the financier had actually placed enormous trust in her by telling her so much. What if she'd gone screaming to the muckrakers? It would be a betrayal of the worst kind.

No, she must continue to tell no one.

After enjoying her soundest sleep in weeks, Helen hurried downstairs to have breakfast. She planned to head to their old house, hoping that her presence there would bring forth an answering appearance by Sean.

"So what is your plan for today—shopping?" asked John Jr.

"Do you think I'd let it go until Christmas Eve to buy my presents for your children?" said Helen in mock horror.

"What *are* you planning to do?" asked Siobhan.

Helen answered, carefully, "I have some errands on 161st Street, not far from the old house. Which brings me to mind: Have you seen it lately?"

His mouth full of eggs, John Jr. said, "Didn't I tell you, Helen? I thought I did. It burned down two years ago. A fireman I know, Jimmy Leeson, got hurt putting it out."

Dismayed, Helen said, "That's terrible. Did the new owner repair the damage?"

"Repair? Nah. It burned down to the foundation, and I heard the man just gave up on it and moved to Queens. I think grass grew over the charred rubble. It's just a vacant lot."

Stephen said, "I didn't think you had such sentimental fondness for the old house, Helen."

"I don't," she said, forcing a neutral expression. When would Stephen stop watching her like a hawk?

Faced with this news, Helen decided not to go to 116th Street after all. She couldn't picture reuniting with Sean over a lot filled with rubble and snow-covered grass. So where should it be—where would Sean look for her?

Within the hour, Helen was on a streetcar bound for Woodlawn. The dance hall always held special meaning for the couple, and throughout their engagement and marriage they liked to ask each other, "What if you hadn't gone with your friend Frances that night?" or "What if you hadn't followed Jerry to the Bronx, looking for new girls to dance with?" It was unlikely Helen and Sean would have ever met if chance decisions didn't place them inside that Woodlawn dance hall.

A disappointment worse than their old house's incineration awaited Helen. The dance hall had long ago been knocked down and replaced by a meat-packing warehouse. It took up half the block in fact. The dance hall had been in sorry shape nearly sixteen years ago, she should have remembered that. How could she think dances were still being given there? Standing outside the warehouse, the stench of butchered meat filling her lungs, she felt sharp regret.

So much of my past with him is torn down, burned, grown over with grass.

There was one place, though, that might not be gone completely.

It was about nine o'clock when Helen began the journey to Brooklyn. It would take a long time to get there—Manhattan was smack in the way. It was difficult to hold onto her euphoria as she managed all the transfers on public transportation. So many people carried packages or boxes of food or wine bottles for Christmas. New York City had a way of turning from ruthlessly competitive to convivial on Christmas Eve. "Have a merry one!" strangers said to one another. But somehow it made

Helen feel more removed from other human beings. She was traveling to a neighborhood where she once lived with her dead husband, hoping his ghost would appear. How festive was that? Not very.

When the subway had made it through most of the length of Manhattan and stopped at Canal Street, just a few stops left before Brooklyn, she almost got off to turn around. Her nerves were so frayed.

But Helen didn't get off the subway. And a few minutes later her car was rattling on the bridge that separated Manhattan from Brooklyn.

After she married Sean, they moved into an apartment over a hardware store in the Brooklyn neighborhood of Windsor Terrace. Ignoring her family's disapproval of such a dwelling, Helen decorated and spruced up every inch of those three rooms. She put effort into each meal she cooked, experimenting with new recipes. Helen never lost her fierce appreciation that this was *theirs*, that she was half of a couple. She wasn't terribly fulfilled by household tasks—that wasn't it. In this marriage she was completely alive, feeling what other young married woman did. Sean responded to her happiness with unflagging devotion, and passion for her slender body.

Not that there was contentment every minute. She knew before they married that Sean was prone to black moods that came out of nowhere, though the moods departed quickly. But she didn't know he was a hypochondriac, fretting over every upset stomach or skin boil in a way her father and brothers never did.

What was surprising, given such fretting, was that Sean had an unfortunate tendency to use his fists when offended. He never raised a finger to Helen. But it was otherwise on the docks of the west side of Manhattan or the shipyards of Brooklyn, where he held a series of laborer jobs alongside his best friend, Jerry, the Belfast Boy redhead who'd led the way at the

Woodlawn dance. Sean was a man who could be provoked. One night he came home drunk, admitting he'd taken a swing at a supervisor who called him "Thick Mick." They tossed him off the docks, swearing it was for good.

Days of unemployment turned into weeks. Jobs were hard to come by, and his friends simply had nothing to offer. They couldn't put in a word. That was why Sean signed up when President McKinley's call went out for soldiers to join the army and fight Spain, promising Helen that he'd be back in a few months with money in his pocket.

"The Irish make the best soldiers," he told his wife. "Didn't we fight for all the New York Yankees in their Civil War, taking the place of the fine gentlemen so they needn't get nicked?"

Just hearing the words "get nicked" filled Helen with fear. She begged Sean to change his mind but to no avail.

"I know how to keep my head down, love," he said, kissing her.

But he didn't know how to survive a deadly disease.

As Helen neared the block where she lived with Sean, she found herself unable to ward off that worst memory of all: her husband's funeral. It was in Brooklyn, arranged by Jerry and two of Sean's cousins in Flatbush, with the Army footing the bill. Helen was of no help with it, for she could barely walk and speech was beyond her. The pain of losing Sean was too hard to bear. What tortured her most was knowing he'd died of typhoid all alone. The longer she lived with Sean, she understood that he was a boy in many ways, a hurt boy sent across the ocean and in doing so leaving his mother behind, his father already dead. He had to fend for himself at the age of fourteen. The loyalty and nurturing love Helen lavished on him were balm to Sean. Whenever he was sick, he clung to her. Typhoid was a horrible way to die. He must have been frightened at the end, without his Helen.

Jerry and his wife, Maggie, did everything they could to

ease Helen's suffering. But it was her three siblings who never left her side, who physically bore her down the church aisle and held her up during the wake. John Jr. was her rock. And so were the others, she acknowledged. When Helen thought about the compassion of Sister Bernadette, who obtained special permission to attend the funeral, or the patience of Stephen, it churned up fresh guilt.

Helen had feared that the Windsor Terrace block too would be destroyed or unrecognizable. But fourteen years later, it stood there, a long brick rectangle.

The hardware store was still open; peering above it, she recognized their window on the second floor facing the street. Helen looked around her. All sorts of people hurried by. Would Sean simply stroll up to her among them? It seemed ludicrous. But she didn't know what else to do but wait.

After more time on the street, she took in that the neighborhood was rundown. The corner store where Sean bought his newspapers and tobacco and liked to joke about football was closed. Across the street stood a sad-looking dentist's office that no one in their right mind would go to.

Moreover, the warmth of the day before had vanished. The temperature was steadily going down to a point more typical of late December. In her euphoric agitation this morning, Helen had run out without gloves or a hat, just her coat flung over a blouse and long skirt. Now she was paying for it. Helen stood outside the store—grappling with her memories, stamping her feet when the cold made her toes ache—and looked up and down the street, without luck. This felt awkward, misconceived.

But I can't give up on Sean so soon.

Helen decided to find a way upstairs to their old apartment and try out some excuse to the people who lived there now. Perhaps Sean would only appear to her inside their home.

The door from the street was unlocked, and she ascended with a tight throat. So many times she'd run up these stairs, her feet flying, laughing at Sean loping behind her. "Slowpoke, slowpoke," she'd taunt, till he leaped those last steps, encircling her with his strong arms and nuzzling her neck.

Helen knocked on the door to their second-floor apartment, but no one answered. She turned the doorknob. It was locked.

Helen sat down on the top step, feeling hollow. She hadn't eaten since seven in the morning, but it was worse than that. This didn't feel right. She longed for a creak on the step to tell her Sean was here, but silence reigned all around her. The stairs were dirty; the smell of ancient cooking grease lingered. An insect crawled up the wall.

Her head dropped into her hands as more memories poured through her. One summer night, lying in bed, she heard Sean's most precious story. "You think you're the special one in this bed, but let me tell you, you may be *aes sidhe*, but I'm descended from kings."

"I know that," she said, resting her head on his chest.

"No, darling, not that kind of king, though I'm happy to hear my wife has no complaints. The O'Neills were once kings of Ireland. My da took me to their coronation place to see it: Tullyhogue."

"Tullyhogue," she repeated, her tongue curling around the word.

"The English smashed it all up a long time ago, but you can still climb the hill. It's in County Tyrone, near Cookstown, about forty-five miles from Belfast. You come to this high hill; it stands above the valley of the River Balinderry. You can see the farms stretching toward these low mountains."

"You're helping me see it too," she whispered, stroking his arm.

"There are some villages below and a few churches. But the best thing is seeing the bogs. I was there in the spring. That's when you see the white flowers that they call Bog Cotton. For all these centuries, people came from far and wide to see this place, *Leac na Ri.*"

She repeated that phrase too, and this time she added her hands, making an outline, using her fingers to illustrate how it sounded to her. She freed her hands when she was with Sean alone, no tamping it down.

"It means 'the flagstone of the kings,' " he explained. "The family that the kings came from was always the same one, the O'Neills. The ceremony was to 'make an O'Neill.' The new king would come forward and sit on this stone chair. He'd be bareheaded, wearing this mantle of frieze cloth that was long, it hung all the way to his knees. When it was over, his supporters would throw a shoe over his head, onto the hill."

"A shoe?" she giggled.

"What—are you making sport of my people? I'll teach you some respect, *aes sidhe.*"

And with that he lifted her on top of him and kissed his wife.

On the steps outside the door where they'd loved each other so passionately, Helen lifted her head. "Sean, are you here?" she said bleakly.

No one answered; no one appeared.

Helen clasped her hands on her lap. She'd known for a while it wasn't the romantic times she missed the most: their first kiss, that day at Coney Island, their wedding night. It was Sean's bad breath in the morning, his cheerful off-key singing at church, and those endless socks to be washed. The ordinariness of their lives together.

Helen shakily got to her feet and walked down the steps to the street.

I can't bear any more of this.

She had nearly reached the subway station when a woman walking toward her in the dimming light stopped and squinted. "Helen?" she asked. Her voice was gravelly.

And distantly familiar. As Helen stared, she realized that she was looking at Jerry's wife, Maggie. She was once a bold chestnut-haired beauty with a throaty voice and a brilliant smile. This woman was gaunt, with a broken front tooth. Her clothes looked shabby.

"I haven't seen you in years," Maggie said. "You never came back to see us."

"No, I am sorry, Maggie—I should have. How are you and Jerry?"

The woman shook her head and pursed her lips as if tasting something foul. "He left me and the kids without a cent to go back to Ireland seven years ago."

"No, oh, no, that's awful," said Helen. "I can't believe it."

Maggie shrugged. She took a step closer to Helen. "I thought you and me would be friends for life, we'd raise our children together."

Helen did not know what to say. It was as if the other woman blamed her for everything.

"You didn't recognize me, did you?" Maggie growled. "You've changed too, but not as bad as me, I guess." Maggie turned away, saying, "You're the lucky one, Helen. Sean would probably have gone back to Belfast too. He talked about it more than any of the fellas, I remember. He could have left you here. This way you never had to go through what I have."

Helen rushed down the subway stairs to escape her.

Her ordeal in Brooklyn was grueling, but the long trip home brought her even lower, the happy holiday greetings among strangers more of a reproach than they were on the way to Brooklyn. A red-faced man, reeking of vodka, bellowed, "Jingle bells, jingle bells, jingle all the way, oh, what fun it is," and then because he didn't know the rest, he repeated that part over and over, his words slurred. Those near him on the subway jammed fingers in their ears. Helen prayed for him to get off the train, and finally he did.

She was utterly exhausted when she made it home, only to be met with a fury of Connolly questions and criticism.

"Where have you been all day?" demanded Stephen. "You come back after ten hours and look, not a single package under your arm."

"I could have used some help getting the house ready for Christmas, Helen," said Siobhan. "We've kept dinner, not knowing where you were."

Helen, struggling to take off her coat, said, "Please, please, no more everyone. I'm sorry. Let's have our dinner."

John Jr. said hesitantly, "There's something you should know first."

"Don't tell her—come now, don't," protested Stephen. "It's impossible."

They exchanged a worried glance, and the weariness that had filled Helen was suddenly gone.

Whatever it is, it's crucial. This is it, I know it, what I've been waiting for.

"Tell me," she pleaded. "What is it?"

"We had the altar boy from St. Michael's come by this afternoon. He said the Dominican friar was there. The message was: Sister Bernadette can see family today, but she said it has to be you who comes."

Helen shoved her arms back into the sleeves of her coat.

Stephen said, "Surely not. It's after five o'clock, too late for the monastery now."

Rose ran across the room, flinging her arms around Helen. "You can't miss the candle! It helps people find their way. You promised you'd do that with me, Aunt Helen. You made a promise!"

"I will do it, I do promise, I will, Rose," Helen babbled, backing toward the door. "I'll be here soon."

With a long walk there and back, she couldn't possibly return "soon." But she needed to see her sister as soon as possible. Her quest to find Sean failed, but at least someone who loved her reached out. Their quarrel would be mended. Sister Bernadette must want it as badly as Helen did, why else send word to her? It was unusual to see family twice in a month, and Christmas Eve seemed an extraordinary time for a nun to be free.

She pushed the door open and ran out onto the street. John Jr. followed her, shouting. "Helen, come back. It's too late."

"Stop telling me what to do," she shouted back. Her outercoat, not buttoned all the way, slapped her legs as she broke into a run.

CHAPTER 10

When Helen reached Corpus Christi Monastery, not only was she half-frozen but also suffering a stitch in her side. It was pitch-black on Lafayette, and no stars twinkled above through the thick clouds. Only the faint lights glowing in the monastery's windows guided her up the path.

Helen banged on the door.

Sweet Jesus, I can barely feel this door—I'm worse off than I realized.

Helen banged a second time and then a third, as no one answered.

Finally, she heard the locks turn. The door opened to reveal a wary nun, about thirty years of age. Another one, older, stood behind her, holding high a lantern so they could get a good look at whomever demanded entry.

"We are not open to outsiders now," the younger nun said firmly.

"My name is Mrs. Helen O'Neill. We had a message today at the house that Sister Bernadette, my sister, could see me."

The nuns looked at each other. "There's been a mistake. No one would have sent a message to family on Christmas Eve. Sister Bernadette has been in service and prayer all day."

"We had a message," Helen insisted. "It came earlier in the day. I'm sorry I didn't come until now. The message was particularly for me." Seeing they were unconvinced, Helen said, "Please, I beg you. Send for her, for Sister Bernadette. She's back there somewhere. Just five minutes."

The nun holding the lantern said, "I'm sorry, but we cannot comply. Absolutely no family messages went out today. If you are in distress, I recommend you seek out your parish priest for assistance."

The door slammed; the key turned.

Bursting into tears, Helen pounded on the door and pleaded for it to be opened. After at least ten minutes went by, she stopped pounding. What choice was there now but to leave?

Helen's head swam. The long walk back home seemed impossible, she was too weak and cold. Too despondent.

How cruel is the world.

J. P. Morgan had been wrong about Memie wanting to help by sending Sean to her. Who knows? Perhaps he misled Helen on purpose. There had been absolutely no sign anywhere of him, not the faintest shadow. Not a whisper.

She laughed wildly in the darkness. When Helen beseeched the underworld to send her back her beloved, the answer was a flat no. Brooklyn was full of pain, her family condemned her, and now the nuns slammed the door in her face rather than permit Sister Bernadette to help.

Helen turned not toward the road but to the far edge of the monastery, finding a trace of the path leading to the cemetery of Corpus Christi. She had no clear or coherent plan, just a thread of a desire pulling her along. She stumbled twice in the darkness but did not fall, and eventually Helen reached the site of the monastics' graves.

She saw the faint outline of the white stone angel between the two trees.

I need to be near her now, the angel. I need her mercy.

She saw movement, like one of the trees swaying. But it wasn't that windy a night.

A tall dark form of a man stepped out from behind the angel.

"About time you favored us with your presence."

It was a voice of Northern Ireland; it was Sean O'Neill. Yet she couldn't make out his face. He was a silhouette.

"Sean," she cried, shaking violently, not trusting her senses. "It's you?" Helen gripped the little gate around the cemetery. This was it—what she'd prayed for so desperately. She felt more frightened than anything else. "I can't see you. It's too dark."

He came toward her, stepping around the tombstones. "The thinking was you would come earlier, Helen."

Now she understood why the nuns so firmly sent her away.

"Did *you* send the friar to the church with the message, Sean? That's why the altar boy said it was only for me?"

"Seemed the best way to do it," he said. "Seeing as I can't very well sit down to dinner with the Connollys."

Sean was almost all the way over to her. That loping stride she knew so well. He held out his arms to embrace her. But suddenly Helen turned her back on him, her hands covering her face. "Don't look at me up close. I'm not pretty, Sean—I'm old!"

"What nonsense. Turn around." He stretched out a hand and, as she quivered with both joy and terror, he laid it on her shoulder. "You'll always be my wee beauty." The hand felt like a human's, it felt like her memory of her husband's touch.

At that Helen stumbled and nearly collapsed, but Sean caught her and lifted her up to stand. Sobs racked Helen's body. She turned her face to his chest. His long arms felt exactly the same as they held her.

"I miss you, I miss you, I never stopped," she wept. "I tried to stop loving you, to give myself some peace, Sean. But I couldn't stop."

"You poor girl, I know, I've watched you. It grieves me to see you like this."

He wore only a trousers and shirt, no coat, and she could feel the fray of his collar. She reached up to touch Sean's face in the darkness, his mouth. She could feel his lips quiver. Was it a smile?

"What was I to you, Helen? The first man to talk you into a walk in the moonlight. You should have recovered from my dying long, long ago."

She struggled in his arms. "How can you say that? How? You knew how I felt."

"I knew it," he said tenderly. "Hush, darling, hush. It's true. The *aes sidhe* feel things deeply."

Sean's voice sounded as if it were coming from far away. Her legs kept buckling. This was what she wanted more than anything else in the world, but she just couldn't take it in, couldn't cope. Why didn't she experience this with the same serenity as J. P. Morgan and Memie? "I think I need to lie down, Sean."

"Whatever you want, Helen." He swooped her up and off her feet, just as he used to, and carried her to the angel. Everything blurred, as if she were falling asleep. When she revived, Helen found herself lying on the ground, her head cradled in Sean's lap. This was better.

"I want to stay with you from now on," said Helen. "Don't make me go back."

"I won't hear that. I don't want that. You think it makes me happy to see my wife grieve like this, to take no pride in what she can do? You've done such wonderful things, Helen. Watching you makes me proud as thunder. You've been earning your pay working for the Yankees, true enough, but some of the grandest Yankees that were ever born."

"It doesn't matter to me, any of that."

"It should, Helen. You're strong and so smart. Much more than me."

Helen reached up and felt his face again, traced the scar above his eye. "Did Mr. Morgan's wife send you to me? Memie?"

"Someone put in a word. Not sure who. Grateful, though."

He's my husband, he truly is. I can feel that sweetness in him, that part of his nature he showed only to me. How can he be a ghost —a ghoul? He's something very different.

"You're no ghost. You're an angel, aren't you, Sean?"

He threw back his head and laughed, and she laughed with him, her heart full. She wasn't frightened any longer.

"I want you to begin to live again, Helen. I'll be watching now. Don't disappoint me, darling. Hear me? I'm still your husband."

She threw her arms around his waist. "Don't leave me."

Something shifted below her; she felt unsteady.

"I have to leave, *aes sidhe.* But remember, I loved you too, more than you knew, more than I ever could put into words."

With that, she felt nothing but the cold, tough ground beneath, her head propped on the marble platform for the angel. He was gone. She should be brokenhearted but instead she felt a distant sadness.

She heard her name. But it wasn't from Sean's lips. It was her brother John Jr., his voice coming from the direction of the monastery.

"Helen, are you here? Helen? Where are you?"

She opened her mouth, but no words came out. A minute went by. It was peaceful here. They might not see her in the darkness, might assume she'd gone elsewhere. She wouldn't be discovered until after sunrise.

Would that be so bad?

"You have to search the cemetery, every inch of it. Because

of her husband, that's where she'd go. Can you see it?" That was Sister Bernadette, she was with John Jr.

And with that, Helen managed to raise her hand.

"Look!" shouted Stephen. "I see her moving over there, under the statue of the angel. She's collapsed."

The voices grew louder, their feet thundered across the ground, and her family surrounded her. Helen looked at them in turn, her two brothers and her sister. "I'm sorry," she said hoarsely.

Sister Bernadette cupped her sister's face with her hands. "Helen, I am the one who's sorry. I didn't understand your pain. I failed you."

John Jr. checked her pulse and ran his hands down her legs. "She may have some frostbite."

A nun and a friar appeared, two people Helen had never seen. They brought blankets and a lantern. Sister Bernadette wrapped Helen in the blanket. Stephen rubbed her hands.

"How ... did you find me?" Helen said.

John Jr. said, "Sister Bernadette told us you visited the cemetery last week, someone saw you. But it was Stephen who said we had to go after you, he was sure that it was a mistake and they would turn you away, and you being in a bad state already. So I went to that Scotsman, Ferguson, and commandeered the motorcar for police purposes. We all drove over, but I had to practically tear the place down to get to Sister."

Stephen laughed. "It was memorable. Your driving—and your tearing down Corpus Christi."

"Yeah, the Bronx police have no jurisdiction—Lord, the mayor has no jurisdiction over this place. You'll be sharing my penance for this, Helen. A thousand Hail Mary's."

Sister Bernadette said, "That's enough of that. What matters is Helen is going to be fine."

"I will be," Helen said. "I will be fine—now." She looked up at Stephen. "You're a good brother to me. I'm sorry for everything."

Stephen murmured, "You *have* to be delirious," but he squeezed her hand.

She heard Siobhan calling: "Did you find her? Is she going to be all right? Can Rose see her?"

"I have to see Rose. Please." Helen tried to sit up, but she was too weak.

John Jr. picked up his youngest sister, wrapped in her blanket, and carried her out of the cemetery, shouting to his wife, "We're coming to you, darling."

As they all made their way up to the main building of the monastery, Siobhan and Rose ran down. "Stop, please, I have to speak to Rose," Helen said. She twisted and turned until she saw the girl at the side of her father and aunt.

"Rose, I am so, so sorry." She reached for her niece. "Your Aunt Helen has been sad and confused. But it's all over now."

"First the doctor," said John Jr.

"I don't need the doctor," Helen said. "I need to light the candle in the window with Rose."

The young girl reached up to grip her aunt's hand. "We'll do it together? We'll wait there to see who needs to come to our home?"

"Yes, love." She gazed at her brothers and sister, and then pressed Rose's hand to her lips. "But you already have the lost person who needs to come home. The person is me."

AUTHOR'S NOTE

John Pierpont Morgan never returned to New York after setting sail for Egypt in January 1913. He died in his sleep in Rome on March 31 of that year at the age of seventy-five, following several strokes. Flags flew half-mast on Wall Street and the stock market closed for two hours. According to biographer Jean Strouse, the congressional hearing, with its harsh criticism of Morgan, probably triggered a mental and physical breakdown.

J. P. Morgan personified the Gilded Age, and Morgan's library, designed by American architect Charles F. McKim, became legendary shortly after it opened in 1906. Hiring Belle da Costa Greene was proof of Morgan's instinct for talent. His son, John Pierpont "Jack" Morgan Jr., saw to it that Belle remained on at the library. In 1924 she was named director of the newly incorporated Pierpont Morgan Library. She died in 1950.

Belle was not in fact Portuguese. Her father was Richard Theodore Greener, the first black graduate of Harvard University. After her father left the family, Belle changed her last name to Greene, added "da Costa," and passed for white. In the context of the time, it was a decision she felt she needed to make.

Morgan's first wife, Amelia Sturges, suffered from tuberculosis when the couple, deeply in love, married in their twenties. He was shattered by her death four months later and some say never completely recovered from the loss.

To learn more about these fascinating people, I recommend the books *Morgan: American Financier* by Jean Strouse; *The House of Morgan: An American Banking Dynasty and the Rise of Modern Finance* by Ron Chernow; *An Illuminated Life: Bella da Costa Greene's Journey From Prejudice to Privilege* by Heidi Ardizzone; and *The Librarian's Office: Inside the Morgan*, by Jennifer Tonkovich, Sidney Babcock, and Noel Adams. I also recommend *The Gilded Age in New York: 1870-1910* by Esther Crain and *Greater Gotham: A History of New York City From 1898 to 1919* by Mike Wallace.

In 1924, Morgan's son opened the Morgan Library & Museum to the public so that everyone could enjoy its beauty. The original studies and libraries as well as the rotunda have been preserved, and wonderful exhibits appear regularly.

Helen O'Neill, Sean O'Neill, and the Connolly family are fictional characters. My telling of the lives of Irish immigrants in America is based on research as well as personal observation. My mother's great-great-grandfather immigrated from County Cork to the United States at the time of the Great Famine. My grandfather, Francis Aloysius O'Neill, struggled to earn an accountant's degree in the 1920s and, finding success, started various businesses in Chicago, Illinois, the city of my birth.

My family is but a speck in the incredible epic drama of the Irish in America. New York City holds a special place: By the end of the 19th century, an estimated one-quarter of the city's residents were Irish. Today Irish Americans make up approximately 5 percent of the population. Morrisania in the Bronx was one of the neighborhoods favored by Irish families in the late nineteenth and early twentieth centuries. Corpus Christi, the oldest Dominican Order for nuns in the United States, still resides in Morrisania, accepting new vocations.

I wish to thank Christine Nelson, the Morgan's Drue Heinz Curator of Literary and Historical Manuscripts, for answering my questions as well as Adam with the Communications & Marketing Department. At the Metropolitan Museum of Art, Ann Bailis, Senior Manager of Media Relations, helped me with questions.

This novella grew out of my longtime love of the Morgan Library & Museum, my wish to write Irish characters in honor of my immigrant roots, and a deep interest in the Gilded Age of New York. It was an email exchange with my writer friend Gaye Mack that put the writing into motion. I apologize to my family for my retreat into a seriously deep writer's cave while I finished it. My special gratitude goes to Elizabeth Kerri Mahon and Emilya Naymark for their contributions to the manuscript. Amy Bruno of HF Virtual Book Tours as always was in my corner. For inspiration, I bow to Kris Waldherr, Joshua James, Mariah Fredericks, Laura Joh Rowland, Laura K. Curtis, Sophie Perinot, Michele Koop, Christie LeBlanc, and Peter Andrews. I'm deeply appreciative of the team at Endeavour Quill for their fine publishing of my novels *The Blue* and *Dreamland*.

Thank you to Sue Trowbridge for helping to create this book and Bosa Grgurevic for designing its cover. And to Max Epstein for agenting my work.

NEXT STOP… DREAMLAND

A NOVEL BY NANCY BILYEAU

Nancy Bilyeau's historical mystery 'Dreamland' is set in 1911 Coney Island.

Read the beginning of *Dreamland*, next page…

Prologue

The phantom city vanished an hour after midnight.

The one million lights of Dreamland darkened as they always did, with a clang as loud as a cannon shot, followed by a long, wheezing gush. The rides, the attractions, the sideshows, the restaurants, the dance halls, the entire fifteen-acre fairground stretching from the Canals of Venice to Lilliput—all of it had been shut down for the night. Once they'd thrown the switch on the light panels, it didn't take long for the heat created by the electric bulbs to dissipate, replaced by the cool, salt-flavored ocean breeze. But the smell of the fairground hung on. Nothing could drive away the scent of stale popcorn, roasted peanuts, taffy and cotton candy, fried crab, boiled corn, and beer, mingling with the odor of greasy machinery and rank human sweat. That was the fragrance of Coney Island, and no one ever forgot it.

The customers trudged home, and the exhausted park workers stumbled to their narrow beds in the apartment houses lining the blocks the other side of Surf Avenue. It was dark and still in the fairgrounds. This was the time when the night policeman made his rounds on the boardwalk. The beach was on his left and Dreamland on his right; the seagulls, his only companions, hopped in the sand.

But then, in the moonlight, he saw the two human figures halfway down the beach, walking slowly toward the water's edge. It was a silhouette of a man, his arm around the waist of a woman wearing a long, dark dress that, in the moonlight, stood out against the white sand. The policeman smiled to himself as the couple sank into the sand. Hadn't he courted his wife the same way? That was twenty years ago, and he still looked forward to coming home, taking off his uniform, and sliding into bed next to her as she slept, the springs creaking as he kissed her soft shoulder.

The policeman kept walking, headed away from the ocean and toward Luna Park, where Shoot-the-Chutes and Helter Skelter were rendered motionless until morning. He didn't hear the woman in the sand: a sharp, startled cry. A few minutes later, there was a different noise: a splash in the water.

No one saw the man walk up the beach and onto the promenade, alone.

~

To order *Dreamland*, go to mybook.to/Dreamland2.

Praise for *Dreamland:*

20 Best Books of 2020, Good Housekeeping Magazine

"Don't sleep on this beautiful novel that twists and turns like the Cyclone through Coney Island. Socialite Peggy is sent to spend the summer there, and she's not happy about it – that is, until she falls in love with one of the artists on the pier. When bodies start piling up in the summer heat, Peggy has to untangle a web of deceit before she or those she loves end up asleep forever."

"Set in the posh hotels and alluring amusement parks of turn-of-the century Coney Island, DREAMLAND is a vibrant maze of desires, scandal, and mystery that pulls you in and doesn't let go. A marvelous book!"
—Ellen Marie Wiseman, bestselling author of *What She Left Behind* and *The Life She Was Given*

"Outstanding thriller... Bilyeau populates her story with achingly believable, realistically flawed characters. Peggy is naive and far from perfect, but her heart is in the right place,

and one can't help feeling for her predicament. This fascinating portrait of the end of the Gilded Age deserves a wide audience."
—*Publishers Weekly* Starred Review

"I could practically taste the salt-water taffy and smell the ocean air as I read Bilyeau's latest, set in 1911 Coney Island. Beautifully written and impeccably researched, DREAMLAND is a rollicking ride."
—Fiona Davis, national bestselling author of *The Dollhouse* and *The Chelsea Girls*

ABOUT THE AUTHOR

Nancy Bilyeau is a historical novelist and magazine editor based in New York. She wrote the Joanna Stafford trilogy, a trio of thrillers set in Henry VIII's England, for Simon & Schuster. Her fourth novel is *The Blue*, an eighteenth-century thriller revolving around the art and porcelain world. Her next novel is *Dreamland*, set in Coney Island of 1911, to be published by Endeavour Quill on January 16, 2020. A former staff editor at *Rolling Stone, Entertainment Weekly*, and *InStyle*, Nancy is currently the deputy editor at the Center on Media, Crime and Justice at John Jay College and contributes to *Town & Country, CrimeReads*, and *Mystery Scene* magazine.

To find out more about her writing projects, learn about giveaways and special offers, and sign up for her newsletter, go to nancybilyeau.com.

ALSO BY NANCY BILYEAU

The Crown

The Chalice

The Tapestry

(the Joanna Stafford trilogy, available through Simon & Schuster)

The Blue

Dreamland

Made in the USA
Monee, IL
01 July 2020

35420434R00069